SONNY'S GIRLS

At Hazelhurst High, Meredith, Cyndi and Jennifer had been football hero Sonny's girls. Now, ten years later, none could forget the night that changed their lives forever.

"That's what scares you, isn't it?"

Nick demanded. "The fact that Sonny was wrong. Your poor, tragic dead hero was wrong. But if you admit how wrong he was, you've betrayed him."

"You've got it all confused," Cyndi said in denial.

"No, you do." With a hand under her chin, he pulled her face up to his. "You didn't bury Sonny. You buried yourself."

She pulled back.

"Kiss me," Nick whispered. "Kiss me and then tell me you don't feel anything. Prove that you're incapable of love."

He lowered his mouth to hers. The kiss was hard, raw. The sensations it roused rocked him to the core.

"How did that feel?" he whispered against her lips. "Like nothing?" Her eyes filled with tears as he stepped backward. "I didn't come here to hurt you, Cyndi." His hand went to her hair. "I never want you to be hurt."

Dear Reader,

Welcome to Silhouette **Special Edition** . . . welcome to romance. Each month, Silhouette **Special Edition** publishes six novels with you in mind—stories of love and life, tales that you can identify with—romance with that little ''something special'' added in.

This month, Silhouette **Special Edition** is full of special treats for you. We're hosting Nora Roberts's third book in her exciting THE CALHOUN WOMEN series—*For the Love of Lilah*. Each line at Silhouette Books has published one book of the series. Next month look for *Suzanna's Surrender* in the Silhouette Intimate Moments line!

Silhouette **Special Edition** readers are also looking forward to the second book in the compelling SONNY'S GIRLS series, *Don't Look Back* by Celeste Hamilton. These poignant tales are sure to be keepers! Don't miss the third installment next month, *Longer Than . . .* by Erica Spindler.

Rounding out August are warm, wonderful stories by veteran authors Sondra Stanford, Karen Keast and Victoria Pade, as well as Kim Cates's wonderful debut book, *The Wishing Tree*.

In each Silhouette **Special Edition**, we're dedicated to bringing you the romances that you dream about— the type of stories that delight as well as bring a tear to the eye. And that's what Silhouette **Special Edition** is all about—special books by special authors for special readers!

I hope you enjoy this book and all of the stories to come.

Sincerely,

Tara Gavin
Senior Editor

CELESTE HAMILTON
Don't Look Back

Silhouette Special Edition

Published by Silhouette Books New York

America's Publisher of Contemporary Romance

For Emilie Richards and Erica Spindler,
my "glorious" partners,
who stuck with me during the rough spots.
Thanks, guys.

SILHOUETTE BOOKS
300 East 42nd St., New York, N.Y. 10017

DON'T LOOK BACK

ISBN: 0-373-09690-9

First Silhouette Books printing August 1991

Printed in the U.S.A.

CELESTE HAMILTON

has been writing since she was ten years old, with the encouragement of parents who told her she could do anything she set out to do, and teachers who helped her refine her talents.

The broadcast media captured her interest in high school, and she graduated from the University of Tennessee with a B.S. in Communications. From there, she began writing and producing commercials at a Chattanooga, Tennessee, radio station.

Celeste began writing romances in 1985, and now works at her craft full-time. Married to a policeman, she likes nothing better than spending time at home with him and their two much-loved cats, although she and her husband also enjoy traveling when their busy schedules permit. Wherever they go, however, "It's always nice to come home to East Tennessee, one of the most beautiful corners of the world."

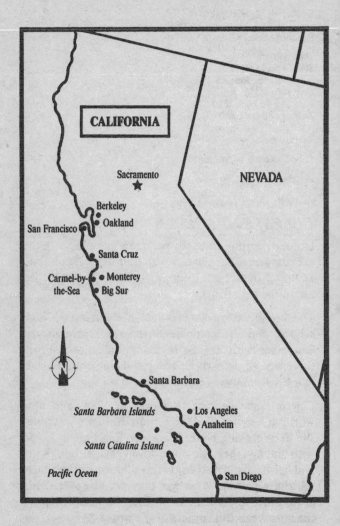

Prologue

The morning wind blew hard off the Pacific, driving sand across the ocean-side parking lot. Fine particles stung Cyndi Saint's legs and peppered her sunglasses until she sought refuge inside her white BMW. Smoothing back her tousled blond hair, she stared at the ocean through weary eyes.

Unable to sleep past dawn, she had driven up the Coast, just as she usually did when she had a problem to think through. She had hoped the wind in her face would force the doubts from her head, would hold the memories at bay. So far, her memories were in retreat. The doubts were another matter.

Get a grip, she told herself. Go home. But she made no move to start the car. Five hours from now she was due back in L.A. for a meeting that would change the course of her professional life. She would have to reply to the network's offer. It was a fabulous offer, a great opportunity.

So why was she hesitating?

Part of the answer was in an envelope on her desk at home. That deceptively innocent rectangle of white paper contained a second notice announcing her ten-year high school reunion.

Ten years. God, what a milestone. A vantage point from which to compare her youthful aspirations with the person she had become. But looking back saddened Cyndi. The comparisons dismayed her. So she had driven away from her memories.

Avoiding them still, she focused instead on the two cars pulling into spaces nearby. Before they rolled to a stop, teenagers erupted from every opening—windows, doors and even a sunroof. The morning air, a moment ago filled only with wind and crashing waves, rang with shouts and laughter. Uninhibited. Full of life. The sounds drew Cyndi, roped her in.

Elbows braced on the steering wheel, she watched the teens pull blankets, towels and coolers from the cars. She counted six kids, no, seven. All attractive. Most as long limbed and bronzed as a Southern California cliché. Yet with the guys roughhousing and the girls giggling, they were just a group of high schoolers, playing hooky, full of high spirits and optimism.

Most of them streamed toward the beach, their shorts and shirts bright neon signals against the sand and water and sky. Near the edge of the parking lot, one girl hung back, holding out her hand to the tallest of the boys. The wind whipped her honey-blond hair across her face, but as the boy caught up to her, Cyndi saw her smile. Who could miss a smile so perfect, so...sure.

The sureness made Cyndi's chest tighten.

For this smiling girl could be her—ten years ago. The handsome boy could be Sonny, and among the others, she would probably find replicas of her high school crowd—brilliant Meredith, bubbly Jennifer, rebellious Ryder. No doubt this girl was as sure of her future as Cyndi had been. For there was a special brand of certainty to be found in being pretty and young and holding hands with the right boy. Having known such false security, Cyndi wanted to chase after the girl, to tell her how quickly things change, how all your certainties can wash away in a month or a day....

Or a single tragic night.

Watching the young couple race across the sand, Cyndi's head filled with memories. She ached for all she had lost. Ten years ago, she had lost Sonny. But more importantly, she had lost her sense of self. At eighteen, when most people questioned the course their life would take, she had been so sure of the future, sure of what she wanted, where she belonged. She had never been so certain since.

"Stop it," she muttered, suddenly impatient with her reflective train of thought. "You have a great life. Stop moping, go back to L.A. and take that new job."

Thus motivated, she started her car and prepared to leave. But the wind carried a burst of laughter through her open window. A glance in her rearview mirror revealed the happy group on the beach. And it took all of Cyndi's strength to avoid the what-might-have-beens that followed as she headed south.

Chapter One

The elevator doors slid to a silent close behind her, but Cyndi stood unmoving, staring at the smoked glass entry to the office at the end of the hall.

Beside her, Lin Redding paused, also. "Well, here we are."

Cyndi nodded, not trusting herself to speak in case her friend guessed how nervous she was. She had tried to compensate for her sleepless night and tiring drive with two bracing cups of coffee, but far from perking her up, the caffeine had left her jumpier than ever about this meeting.

Even Lin, normally cool under pressure, seemed inclined to hesitate. "Let's remember they came to us," she told Cyndi.

"Right. The network offered us a new show."

"Because we're good."

"Yes, you're a great director, Lin."

"I'm only as good as the talent I direct."

Beginning to feel calmer, Cyndi acknowledged the compliment with a smile. "I guess we're just a mutual admiration society."

"Deserved admiration," Lin retorted. "We wouldn't be standing here if *Cyndi Saint's Aerobic Shape-Up* wasn't more than just another cable-TV exercise show. We're ready to move on."

Cyndi wished she could be as sure of the future as Lin sounded. Part of her wanted things to stay exactly as they were.

For two years, their show had been one of the Choice Channel Cable Network's most popular daytime programs. She credited most of the success to the rapport she and Lin had established from the start. Lin's innovative direction gave the show the sleek look of a music video; Cyndi concentrated on developing new routines that blended low-impact aerobics with simple but fun dance steps. She loved the work. She wasn't nearly so confident about the network's new offer.

But Lin looked as if she had conquered her momentary qualms. They started down the hall. "Let's get in there and accept that offer." Only in front of the network programming chief's office door did Lin hesitate again, stopping to smooth a hand through her dark hair. "Do I look okay?"

"Of course," Cyndi assured her, although "okay" was an understatement when it came to Lin's exotic looks. She was tall and slim like her Nebraska corn-farmer father, with the delicate features and dark hair of her Vietnamese mother. Her eyes were closer to green than brown, the color seeming to change with her emotions. Standing beside Lin, Cyndi always felt as if her own blue-eyed blondness was pale and ordinary.

That feeling was heightened by her continued edginess. Telling herself to relax, Cyndi straightened the collar of her jade suit and squared her shoulders. Yet when the receptionist swung open the doors to Harris Fielding's inner sanctum, she felt as anxious as Dorothy facing the great and powerful Oz. That was ridiculous, considering Harris, with his sad eyes and shaggy hair, had always reminded her of a bassett hound.

The stranger beside Harris, however, had the look of a wolf.

He claimed Cyndi's complete attention as she walked across the room. He wasn't handsome, this man. His dark hair was unruly. His face was lived-in, with thick, slightly arched eyebrows and a long, rather crooked nose. Time had placed creases beside his eyes and mouth and combed the dark hair at his temples with gray. Not tall, he appeared nonetheless powerful. Not handsome, he was still the sort of man women would look at twice. *Some* women, Cyndi amended, eyeing the wrinkles in his gray suit. She preferred men with a little more polish. Men without such dark, predatory eyes.

Turning from the man, Cyndi greeted Harris Fielding, who came around his desk and took her hand. Harris was his usual effusive self, full of compliments. Beaming with pride at Cyndi and Lin, he introduced the stranger as Nick Calderaro, the new executive in charge of daytime programming, the man who would be developing their new show.

Startled, Cyndi darted a glance at Lin, who betrayed similar surprise. Their cable network was a small operation in comparison to the big broadcast channels. Nick Calderaro was assuming a newly created position.

Calderaro came forward, nodding. "Ladies," he said, taking Lin's hand first and smiling. "I like your work, Miss Redding."

He turned to Cyndi. His smile never slipped, but her chest tightened nevertheless. She was used to male scrutiny, but not the disapproval in this man's gaze. "Miss Saint," he said, his handshake firm yet brief.

Murmuring his name, she waited, thinking he would elaborate with the same sort of comment he had made to Lin. But he was silent. He studied her long and hard, until she felt angry heat sting her cheeks. What a rude man.

With customary cheeriness, Harris's voice rang out. "Let's all have a seat and get down to business, okay?"

Calderaro didn't join Cyndi and Lin on the chairs in front of Harris's desk. Arms crossed, he perched on the broad window ledge to the right. And still he gazed at Cyndi. His attention angered her further, but she stubbornly focused on what Harris was saying.

He repeated the pitch he had made to Lin and Cyndi last week. Lin was being offered executive producer status of a program the network envisioned as a daily health, beauty and fitness magazine. Cyndi would host the show, tying together segments and interviewing guests. The network wanted her as host, not only because of the success of her other show, but because market research had shown her to be well liked by the target female audience.

Sounding excited by the show's prospects, Harris leaned forward. ''We want to build an entire afternoon around this noontime show. Cyndi, Lin, there's a lot riding on your shoulders.''

Cyndi could see Lin's response to the challenge. She straightened her back. Her eyes flashed. Of course she wanted this. And if Lin wanted it, if she thought Cyndi could do it—

''Think you're up to it, Miss Saint?''

Calderaro's voice cut Cyndi's burgeoning excitement back to a nub. ''Pardon?'' she managed to say, trying to buy some time.

His steady regard didn't waver from her face. His tone was even as he repeated, ''I asked if you thought you could do this show.''

Leather squeaked as Harris shifted in his chair. ''Nick, I told you the network has the utmost confidence in Cyndi.''

''I asked her what she thought.''

Struggling for just the right answer, Cyndi managed what she hoped was a bright smile. All her life she had used this smile to cover up doubts or fears or insecurities. With her mother watching her lead cheers at school. While walking down the aisle at her wedding. Signing her divorce papers. Taping her first exercise video. Her smile had always been her shield.

Now she turned up the wattage for Nick Calderaro's benefit. "I'm excited by this offer—"

"That's not what I asked," he interrupted in the same calm but challenging tone. "You're not a journalist. You have little experience with interviews. Aren't you worried about making this concept work?"

Lin sat forward. "We've incorporated a lot of the elements you're worrying about into our current show. Cyndi's gone on location, had guests—"

Finally moving from his negligent pose by the window, Calderaro brushed Lin's comments aside by a wave of his hand. "I've spent the last couple of days reviewing tapes of your show, Miss Redding. I know what Miss Saint has done in the past. I'm only interested in what she can do next."

Cyndi stiffened. "You don't sound as if you have much confidence in me, Mr. Calderaro."

"Right now I'm interested in your assessment of your abilities. You're the one who has to do this job."

He looks at me as if he knows what a fraud I am, Cyndi thought. She rubbed suddenly damp palms across her skirt while anger and confusion warred inside her. Anger won. She closed her hands into fists and met Calderaro's gaze straight on. "I'm sure the network wouldn't be offering me a job they didn't think I could do."

"Maybe. Maybe not."

Harris cut in, "Come on, Nick..."

Calderaro turned, laughing carelessly. "Harris, you and I know this network, not unlike others we've worked for, really only cares about impressions, and that hasn't much to do with reality." He looked back at Cyndi. "Their *impression* of you, their viewers' *perception* of you is that of an attractive, likable woman." He stepped closer to her chair and sat on the edge of the desk, crossing his arms again. "You've got a beautiful face, a great body..." His gaze slipped over her as his voice deepened. "And the camera loves every inch of you."

It was a peculiar talent, Cyndi decided, the way his pleasant tone could still turn a compliment into an insult. She could feel her face growing hot again.

Harris interceded on her behalf. "Just hold on a minute, Nick. The network—" he paused, adding emphasis to his next words, *"—the same network that is your new employer,* thinks Cyndi has much more to offer than her looks."

"She's already proven that," Lin said. Cyndi sent her a grateful smile.

But one brief movement of Calderaro's shoulders displayed his opinion of what Cyndi had proved.

She wanted to slap him. Or walk out. Or take up the gauntlet he had so clearly thrown down. Surprisingly it was the last emotion that exerted the most pull. She pushed herself out of her chair. That put her a little taller than Calderaro, who still sat on the desk's edge. She liked the feeling of superiority. "I can do this program," she said evenly. "I can do it well."

He stood, and they faced each other. He still wasn't much taller, but Cyndi felt dwarfed. She struggled not to step back.

"I'm excited about this opportunity," she heard herself say, wondering where the confidence in her voice had come from. "I'll admit it's different from what I've done so far in my career. But I'm ready for it."

A smile curved Calderaro's mouth. For the first time since walking into the room, Cyndi thought she had pleased him. "It isn't going to be easy," he murmured. "I won't make it easy."

"Good." The word slipped out before she could think, but she liked the way she sounded. "I don't want anyone doing me any favors. Especially not you."

He laughed then and finally took a seat, allowing Harris to take command of the meeting again. Preparation for the new show would begin almost immediately. Cyndi nodded and made what she hoped were appropriate responses. She would have to get the details from Lin later. Her head was throbbing so hard she couldn't concentrate on anything.

Anything but Nick Calderaro.

His challenging little smile disconcerted her. Reminded her of someone. Made her certain she would let him down.

Already questioning the wisdom of what she had gotten herself into, she was happy when the meeting ended.

Nick was surprised by being disappointed when Cyndi and Lin left. In fact, he stared at the doors for a few moments after they had disappeared.

Only a groan from his boss made Nick turn back to the business at hand. "Lord, Nick," Harris said, dropping into his chair. "Did you have to be so hard on her? What if she had told us to take a flying leap?"

Nick loosened the knot on the tie that had been choking him for the past hour. "I was sort of hoping she would quit," he muttered. "Then we could have gotten a pro to take on the job."

"And the top brass could have had your job before it began."

"Wouldn't be the first time I was fired," Nick returned, grinning. "As I recall, we were both 'let go' on the same day one time back in New York."

Though Harris pretended annoyance, Nick saw the telltale twitch of his lips. "Well, I want to keep this job," he said finally. "In the fifteen years since this wonderful world of television brought us together, I've acquired a wife and three kids."

Nick paused in the act of sitting down. "Three? When did you get a third?"

"On a rainy night about two years ago," Harris replied, laughing. "You ought to try starting a family. It would keep you in the same job for more than a year."

"Hey, I'm planning on staying here with you for a while. I wouldn't let a pal down."

"And I have no doubt the Calderaro genius will do wonders for the daytime lineup. But you've got to promise to control your contempt for network favorites like Cyndi Saint."

Nick shrugged. "You knew my opinion before she walked in the door today."

"She'd been approached about the show before you decided to take me up on my offer." A frown drew Harris's shaggy eyebrows together. "I have to admit I had a few qualms about her myself at first."

"Then why hire her?"

Harris smiled wryly. "Even though I am head of programming, there are other people around here who have some say in the decisions."

Grunting in disapproval, Nick said, "You've learned to play the corporate game, haven't you, old friend?"

"I've learned to be flexible," Harris corrected. "I'm flexible enough to give Cyndi Saint a chance."

"But you told me you wanted this show to be slick. Do you honestly think she can handle it?"

Harris shrugged. "She works hard. She has good camera presence. She seems to learn fast. And she has desire."

"Does she?"

"She told you she wanted the job."

"Yeah, after I pushed her to the wall."

"That should have proven something. It takes someone with backbone to stand up to Nick Calderaro's scorn."

Unsettled by Harris's choice of words, Nick frowned. "I wasn't scornful, was I?"

"No more than you usually are with beautiful, ambitious blondes."

Thoughtfully Nick rubbed his chin. Cyndi Saint was beautiful. Peaches-and-cream complexion. Hair like sunshine. Body honed to slender perfection. "Beautiful and ambitious," he murmured. "They're always that way, aren't they?"

He didn't listen to Harris's response. He was thinking instead about the contradiction he had read in Cyndi Saint today. There was something vulnerable about the woman. It had been in her expression when she walked into the room and again when he had asked her if she could do the job. In his experience, vulnerability had little to do with beautiful, ambitious blondes. Women like that were made of plastic, too hard edged for the softer emotions. He didn't think Cyndi Saint had that sort of edge. Not yet, anyway. But he didn't hold out any hope for her. He knew time and this business would file her softness into a spiny, sharp shell.

"A pity," he muttered, remembering the uncertainty that briefly clouded her beautiful blue eyes. That flash of emotion had made her human. Too bad it would disappear.

Hitting the button that opened her garage door, Cyndi muttered, "Maybe I can just disappear." She guided her car into its space next to her brother's car. "I'll get on a plane for South America. The network will fire me. I'll never have to do this show or see Nick Calderaro again."

The unlikeliness of that happening was underscored by the garage door as it rattled to a close behind her. There was no escape. Cyndi, who hated change, was making a big one.

Leaning her head against the steering wheel, she thought about Lin's excitement. Her friend had been impressed with the way Cyndi had stood up to Nick Calderaro. Lin had heard of him, said he was a television genius who had worked in almost every phase of the business—from news to programming to advertising. He had even directed a couple of music videos. He was a maverick. A demanding perfection-ist.

"Just what I need in my life," Cyndi moaned.

As a knock sounded on her car window she jumped and looked up into her brother's frowning face. She rolled down the window. "Devlin, you scared the life out of me."

"Why are you sitting in the car?"

"I accepted the network's offer."

"Oh." Sagely Devlin nodded, his blond hair slip-ping over his forehead. "Now I see why you look so upset. Must be tough to get your own talk show, especially when your bosses give you a big raise and—"

"Just cut it out," Cyndi said, jerking the door open. "You don't understand."

"Nope, I don't." Devlin swung his jacket over his shoulder as Cyndi climbed out of the car. "You should be celebrating."

"You sound like Lin." Cyndi's friend had begged her to come out for a celebratory dinner. Yearning for privacy in which to worry, Cyndi had declined.

"That woman is good for you. You spend too much time alone."

"Yes, yes, I know," Cyndi agreed irritably. This was an old argument between her and her brother. Devlin was a supremely social creature. He had never understood Cyndi's reserve. She had few friends, particularly female friends. Not since high school . . . no, she corrected herself, even then she wasn't close to other girls. Her mother had always blamed it on jeal-ousy over Cyndi's looks and told her that girls didn't matter anyway. With Lin, Cyndi at last had what she considered a close friend. Her mother, if she were alive, probably wouldn't believe the lack of rivalry between them.

Irreverently Devlin ruffled Cyndi's hair. "Congratulations, anyway. Try not to mope about it too much tonight."

Cyndi had to smile. "You know me too well, little brother."

"Sorry I can't stick around to share your gloom, but I'm due at the hospital." Still grinning, he started toward his car. "The job's not glamorous—not like being a television personality—but someone has to do it."

"Ah, the sad plight of a poor overworked intern," Cyndi teased, leaning on her opened door. "Especially one who crashes regularly at his sister's home. Soaks in her hot tub. Uses her towels. Eats her food."

"That reminds me—I left you a list of everything we need from the market," Devlin said as he got into his car. He opened the garage door and started the engine.

Cyndi's indignant response was drowned in the roar of his car's engine. In the kitchen she found a grocery list, written in the illegible scrawl seemingly required of all doctors, propped against an empty milk container on the kitchen counter.

"That boy will never change," she murmured, although she knew there were women who might have laughed at her calling Devlin a boy. But surely an older sister could be forgiven for continuing to think of her brother in such terms. Back home, she and Devlin had been mortal enemies. He was two years younger, a mischievous scamp who had bedeviled her until she'd left for college and married. Only when he had started medical school here in L.A. had they become close. He had his privacy in the unused bedroom and bath down on the garage level. After her divorce it had been especially nice to have Devlin around her house.

Her house. The words made Cyndi smile as she dropped her purse onto the square pine table in the middle of the kitchen. The house had become hers after the divorce. Although it had actually been hers before then. Her ex-husband had thought it too small and not flashy enough for a rookie football player bound for stardom. But Cyndi had loved this place from the beginning, loved the stuccoed walls and Mexican-tiled floors, loved the little walled garden off her bedroom and the atrium window here in the kitchen. She had insisted on buying this house, one of the few things she had insisted on during her brief marriage. Here, she had dared to dream of children, of a station wagon, of dance lessons and baseball practice, of all the trappings of the nice, normal life she wanted. She had even bought a cat.

As if on cue, an orange-and-white bundle of fur came slinking around the corner. The cat proceeded to rub against cabinets and appliances before deigning to flick Cyndi's leg with its tail.

Laughing, Cyndi stooped to stroke her pet. "Yes, Lolita, dear girl, at least I still have you and the house. I never really had the husband. I certainly don't have the dreams I once had."

But as she headed for her bedroom, Cyndi pushed aside the annoying thought that her dreams hadn't really changed. She would still like to have those children, the station wagon, that simple, ordered life. She had certainly never intended to get into television.

"It was an accident," she told Lolita, who had assumed her usual regal pose in the middle of Cyndi's bed. "My whole life is just one big accident."

The memory of Nick Calderaro's challenging smirk taunted her.

As her head began to pound again, Cyndi kicked off her shoes and thought longingly of a nice long soak in the hot tub. But her gaze was drawn to the desk in the corner, where the invitation to her high school reunion still lay. Unable to resist, she picked up the letter.

Hazelhurst High. Idly her thumb stroked over the engraved letterhead. As she scanned the letter again, she sank to the edge of the bed. She wouldn't go to the reunion, of course. She had left behind what had happened ten years ago.

Or had she? For just when she thought she had forgotten, the memories always came back, inspired by a decade-old song playing on the radio or a glance at an old photograph. And just as she had done early this morning, Cyndi always tried to run away from those memories. Yet she never got away. No matter how she tried to forget what had happened, she couldn't avoid the facts. Ten years ago her life had started veering off course; she had never been able to set it straight again. She had never become the person she had intended to be, the person she was supposed to be.

Lolita moved down the bed and nuzzled Cyndi's hand, a rare sign of affection. But Cyndi ignored her. She told herself to get up, get busy, to avoid the temptation to look back. But she couldn't. Especially since she now realized who Nick Calderaro's challenging smile reminded her of. He made her think of Sonny.

Sonny, her first love. Sonny, who had challenged her, taunted her, pushed her, confused her. Sonny, whom she had failed.

Cyndi tried to stop the scenes that were clicking through her head, scenes from those last months of high school. She remembered all the events she had managed to avoid thinking of this morning at the beach. She thought of her mother, whom she had tried so hard to please. Of Meredith and Jennifer, the two girls who might have been her friends if she had known how to reach out to them. Of that horrible night when everything with Sonny had changed. What had happened that night had affected every choice she had made since.

Even more painful than that night, however, was what had come before. Those shining moments before her perfect world had exploded.

"I don't want to remember," she whispered, closing her eyes.

But when she opened them again, she was staring at the roses in a painting on the wall. They were deep pink—the same color as the dress she had worn to the prom....

Chapter Two

All Those Years Ago...

Holding the unhooked bodice of her gown tight against her, Cyndi did a quick turn. The full taffeta skirt crackled, a mere whisper against her legs as it skimmed the dressing room's walls. Closing her eyes, she envisioned herself at the prom, dancing with Sonny, the deep rose of her dress swirling against his black tuxedo.

"Cyndi?" Her mother's precise tones, edged with impatience, intruded on her daydreams. "Come out. Let's see this dress."

This dress. Fran Saint's preconceived opinion of the formal her daughter had chosen was clear. Defiantly Cyndi raised her chin. For once, her mother was wrong.

"Cyndi? We're waiting." Even though Cyndi knew the owner of Sinclair's Dress Shoppe was hovering nearby, Fran now made no attempt to hide her exasperation. "I don't have all afternoon."

Knowing she could stall no longer, Cyndi stepped out.

Mrs. Sinclair's tightly permed red hair bounced as she clapped her hands. "Beautiful, Cyndi, just beautiful. Don't you think so, Mrs. Saint?" Her desire to please Fran, a doctor's wife who was influential in the small town's social circles, was painfully obvious.

But Cyndi's mother said nothing as she surveyed her daughter.

"Well, what do you think?" Cyndi demanded breathlessly.

Before Fran could reply, Mrs. Sinclair hurried Cyndi toward the dais and many-sided mirror at the opposite end of the spacious pink-and-white fitting area. "Let's get you zipped and into your shoes and jewelry so your mother will get the whole effect."

But the shop owner was called out of the dressing room before Cyndi could do more than slip on satin pumps dyed to match the dress. So it was Fran who, silently, zipped and hooked and straightened the dress. And scrupulously Cyndi avoided looking in the mirror. She couldn't bear it if the dress wasn't right, after all.

She and her mother had argued more about this dress than they had argued about anything, ever. Weeks ago, during a trip to Fran's favorite exclusive shops in nearby Columbus, Ohio, Cyndi had rejected every gown she was offered. For the biggest night of her life, she wanted to choose her own dress, rely on her own taste. And without her mother's help, she had found exactly what she wanted, right here in Hazelhurst, Ohio's best dress shop.

Hazelhurst's best wasn't usually good enough for her mother, but Fran had said nothing about the purchase until today, when Cyndi was scheduled for a final fitting to check the alterations. Now, as Fran smoothed out a crease in the formfitting midriff, Cyndi wished her mother wasn't so picky, so...perfect.

But she was. Fran was the same slender size she'd been on her wedding day some twenty years ago. Her hair was as blond as her daughter's, her skin as firm and smooth. Her makeup was always flawless, her attire flattering. Today, for a simple trip to downtown Hazelhurst, she was elegant in lilac silk sweater and matching slacks. Diamonds sparkled at her ears and around the face of her wristwatch.

Her mother bent forward to hook the dress, and Cyndi breathed in the subtle sweetness of her perfume. The scent was familiar because it lingered in every room at home, stamping the entire house with Fran's personality. More than once Cyndi had wished their house smelled like just-baked cookies, as her friend Jennifer's always did. Or soap-and-water clean like Meredith's. And, traitorously, she had wished for a mother who was a little less perfect, a little more like the mothers of her friends.

Wishing that now, Cyndi tugged on white lacy gloves. With cool fingers, Fran settled the strand of pearls against Cyndi's neck. "There, I guess this is the *whole effect.*"

Ignoring the subtle dig at nice Mrs. Sinclair, Cyndi looked in the mirror. Her glance traveled expectantly from the floor to tanned shoulders left bare by her upswept hair and the dress's neckline. Then, heart hammering, she looked at her mother, who stood to the side, studying her daughter's reflection.

"It's fine," Fran murmured before turning away. "Almost as pretty as the white dress in Columbus."

A pain stabbed Cyndi's chest, a hurt so intense she had to catch her breath. Why, she wondered, why was her mother's approval so important? Choosing her own dress was a small thing, but she had hoped it would prove she could make some of her own decisions, that she wasn't completely under her mother's thumb, as Sonny contended. But she hadn't proved anything. Except, perhaps, how very much her mother's opinion really did matter.

Pleasing Fran Saint wasn't easy. She had high expectations for her children. Her son, Devlin, delighted in bucking her at every turn. But Cyndi usually wanted those things her mother wanted for her, like being a cheerleader, wearing pretty clothes and dating Sonny Keighton, the most popular boy in school. Most especially, Cyndi had wanted Sonny. And of all her accomplishments, Sonny pleased her mother best.

So what will she do if you lose him?

Cyndi's eyes grew wide as she considered the question she had been ignoring during these past, unsettled weeks with Sonny. She told herself to ignore it now. She and Sonny were meant for each other. Everyone said so. In the fall they would go to college together. Later on, they would get married and Sonny would follow in his father and grandfather's footsteps at the bank. Cyndi had mapped out a smooth path to the future. It was a future she knew would please her parents. It was what she wanted. She would make it come true, no matter what she had to do to hold Sonny.

No matter what.

The words seemed to echo inside her head.

"Cyndi! Oh, my gosh, your dress is *gorgeous.*"

There was no mistaking the dramatic phrasing or the husky voice of one of Cyndi's best friends. Cyndi turned to find Jennifer Joyce standing in the fitting room doorway, her arms overflowing with peach-colored ruffles. As usual, her infectious smile coaxed a grin from Cyndi.

"Do you really like it?" Darting a quick glance at her mother, Cyndi held her skirt out and did a quick spin.

"Like it? I *love* it." Jennifer dumped her arm load of ruffles in a chair and, looking exasperated, raked a hand through her feathery auburn bangs. "If only I could have found a dress that perfect."

Fran's smile was cool. "Jennifer, dear, I'm sure your dress is lovely. Shouldn't you hang it up?"

Rather sheepishly, Jennifer retrieved the dress and hung it on a dressing room door. "I don't know what Ryder's going to say about this dress."

"Ryder?" Fran echoed. "Do you mean Ryder Hayes?"

"Mother," Cyndi chided. "I told you Jennifer was going to the prom with Ryder."

And though Fran said nothing, Jennifer's cheeks grew pink. "Ryder's not so bad, Mrs. Saint."

Fran crossed to the chair where she had left her purse. "I'm sure he isn't if you like him, Jennifer."

"It's just his motorcycle," Jennifer continued, her brown eyes flashing. "People see it and think the worst."

Loyally Cyndi added, "Mother, I've told you how nice Ryder is when Sonny and I double with him and Jennifer." That much was true. What she hadn't told her mother was how much Ryder supposedly smoked and drank and how often he was in trouble at school— usually for smarting off. Those were things Fran wouldn't want to know about the boy who was Sonny's best friend, a boy she already disliked, just because he came from The Creek, Hazelhurst's least desirable neighborhood.

Fran took a slim gold compact from her purse. "I only hope Ryder Hayes appreciates having you girls jump to his defense."

Jennifer looked startled for a moment but said nothing more. She frowned as she toyed with a ruffle on her dress.

The sudden tension in the dressing room made Cyndi uneasy. It was always like this when her mother was around her friends. She and Jennifer and their fellow cheerleader, Meredith Robbins, had been rivals for many honors at school. Cyndi would have been lying if she said she had never felt the competition among the three of them, but her mother seemed to feel it more. Right now, she was probably congratulating herself because Cyndi was dating Sonny instead of Ryder. Cyndi wondered what her mother would say if she knew what reckless impulses Sonny shared with his friend.

That thought brought up issues Cyndi didn't want to deal with at the moment, so she turned back to the mirror. "Will you unzip me, Jennifer?"

"Sure." Jennifer moved up on the dais beside Cyndi. "But Meredith's with me and she'll want to see your dress."

Only moments later Meredith burst into the dressing room. And that was a surprise, because calm, even-tempered Meredith, the smartest person in Hazelhurst High, rarely *burst* in anywhere. But today she was in a rush, tossing her long brown hair over her shoulder, her cheeks glowing as she said, "Jennifer, you've got to come outside. Ryder and Sonny are—" Drawing up short, Meredith's blue eyes looked into Cyndi's and then swung away. "Cyndi. Mrs. Saint." She nodded at Cyndi's mother. "I didn't realize you were here."

Jennifer claimed her attention. "Don't you just love Cyndi's dress?"

Meredith scanned Cyndi from head to toe, but still didn't meet her gaze. She smiled, however, a thin, nervous smile that left Cyndi wondering what was wrong. She and Meredith hadn't had a real conversation in weeks.

Fran closed her compact with a firm little click. "Meredith, are you trying on your dress, too?"

"Mother and I got my formal in Columbus."

Cyndi and her mother shared the briefest of glances. Fran's pretty mouth tightened. Cyndi looked away. "Meredith, did you say Sonny was out front?"

"With Ryder."

Anxious for Fran to be gone, Cyndi asked her to tell Sonny she wanted a ride home. Her mother agreed; she was always happy for Cyndi to be with Sonny. Nodding to the other girls, Fran disappeared into the shop. Cyndi turned back to the mirror, cocking her head to the side as she studied her formal. *It is perfect,* she told herself. *No matter what Mother thinks.*

Lightly Jennifer touched Cyndi's skirt, a wistful look in her eyes. "Has Sonny seen your dress?"

"Not yet." Cyndi didn't want him to see her until the prom next Saturday.

"You two will look great together. As usual." Sighing, Jennifer went to the dressing room where her formal was hanging. "Meredith, won't Cyndi and Sonny look just right?"

Meredith barely had a chance to reply before Jennifer was going on about the prom and decorations and upcoming graduation festivities. In fact, Jennifer's steady flow of conversation almost made up for the fact that Meredith had nothing to say. She helped Cyndi out of her dress; she zipped and fastened Jennifer's. But she was unusually quiet.

Even though Meredith was never a chatterbox like Jennifer, her silence bothered Cyndi. She wished she could ask her what was wrong. Just as she longed to squeeze Jennifer's hand and find the right words to reassure her about the frilly, fluffy peach formal that somehow transformed the gamine tomboy into a beauty. But Cyndi knew Meredith would dismiss her concern. Jennifer would be embarrassed by too much praise. And that saddened Cyndi.

These were supposed to be her best friends, but she talked to them about nothing deeper than cheerleading routines, lipstick colors and homework. Unlike the friends in books Cyndi had read, they never shared their darkest fears or deepest longings. Sure, she knew Meredith was going to Vassar, where she would undoubtedly set the academic world on its ear with her brilliance. She knew Jennifer preferred to stay near home and attend a junior college. And of course, both of them knew Cyndi planned to marry Sonny. Yet Cyndi didn't even consider telling them about the arguments she and Sonny had been having. They never talked about problems.

Because none of us are supposed to have problems, Cyndi thought as she stepped out of the dressing room and settled a pink zippered bag over her formal. Without being vain, Cyndi knew she and Meredith and Jennifer were Hazelhurst High's most popular senior girls. They were cheerleaders, organizers, trendsetters. They came from good families with nice homes. Their futures were secure. They weren't supposed to have a care in the world.

But their reflections in the fitting room mirror told a different story. Cyndi traded her pearl necklace for a chain holding Sonny's class ring and studied her own worried expression. To one side Meredith leaned against a wall, arms folded across her slender waist, her eyes big and blue and unmistakably sad. Even Jennifer, the happiest person Cyndi knew, now wore a frown, her chatter having faded to nothing. They were all silent. Yet the very air crackled with some unspoken anxiety. Cyndi could only compare them to a group of strangers waiting for a train. Waiting and waiting, keeping their frustrations quiet, ready to explode.

She was the first to bolt. Forcing a smile for her friends, she collected her dress and other belongings. Outside, Sonny waited. Through the shop window she could see his blond hair gleaming in the sunshine. And when he turned to greet her, his perfect smile lighting his even features, Cyndi felt her puzzling tension ease. The world was right when Sumner Franklin Keighton III smiled.

He slid from his perch on the hood of the sporty red car he'd parked in the No Parking zone in front of Sinclair's. "Hey, Princess."

She smiled at the nickname, one he had bestowed on her in fifth grade, when she had played Sleeping Beauty in a school pageant. He had been Prince Charming, of course. The label could apply now, since the handsome boy had become a tall, well-built eighteen-year-old. A man, he said often.

He stashed her dress bag across the car's back seat. "Where've you been? Ryder and I were starting to think you weren't even in there."

"Didn't Mother tell you—"

"Yeah, yeah." His aquamarine eyes clouded. "Your mother gave me orders to wait." Sonny's dislike of Fran Saint was a fairly recent development, one he elaborated on in private to Cyndi but hid from Fran and most everyone else.

She didn't bother nagging him about his attitude; they had disagreed about her mother too many times in recent weeks. She turned instead to Sonny's companion, who continued to lean against the car. "Ryder, Jennifer's inside, too."

"So I see." Ryder nodded toward Jennifer's compact car.

"Meredith, too," Cyndi said, unnecessarily.

Ryder grinned, the slow, lazy smile that always made Cyndi feel he knew a secret about her. "Oh, yes," he said, turning his face up to the sun. "The gang's all here."

Something about the statement jarred Cyndi, but she couldn't think of an appropriate comeback, as was invariably the case with Ryder. She wasn't sure why he and Sonny were such good friends. They were opposites in so many ways—even down to their looks. Today Ryder's tattered cutoffs and T-shirt contrasted with Sonny's country-club-neat tennis shorts and pullover. But it didn't seem to matter to Sonny that Ryder had little money or that his father was a drunk. In fact, Sonny was the one who seemed to delight in Ryder's friendship.

Cyndi admired and tried to emulate Sonny's generous spirit. His ability to get along with so many different people was what made him so popular. Her father said Sonny should plan a career in politics instead of banking. Whatever he did, Cyndi just wanted to be at his side. She was Sonny's girl. Always had been. Always would be.

She heard Jennifer call out. Ryder dropped his bored pose and pushed a hand through his too-long, dark hair. Meredith came out of the store at a slower pace, but soon all of them were clustered on the sidewalk around Sonny. Just like on the football field, he started calling the plays.

"Let's go up to the summer house." He referred to his parents' place on Crystal Lake, just outside of Hazelhurst.

"Yes, let's do," Jennifer agreed. "It's hot enough to swim."

Cyndi hesitated, glancing at the wristwatch whose wide band matched her fuchsia shorts. "It's kind of late—"

"Oh, don't be a drag, Princess." This time, the emphasis Sonny put on her nickname was less than pleasing, and his smile had become a challenge. A familiar challenge, Cyndi realized, just as pushing her to do something she didn't want had become a familiar routine with Sonny.

Momentary hurt squeezed through her. She didn't want to be a "drag," but she also didn't want to go to the lake. Eventually everyone would leave, and she and Sonny would be alone. On one hand, being alone with him was all she wanted. On the other, there was this little voice inside of her—her mother's voice—which told her what was going to happen when they were alone. The same voice said it couldn't happen. And in the confusion between what Sonny wanted, what Cyndi felt and what she knew was right, she knew there would be another argument. And she didn't want to argue with him. She loved him....

To her relief, Meredith spoke up. "I can't go."

Sonny turned his most wheedling smile on her while he casually draped an arm around Jennifer's shoulders. "Isn't anybody but J.J. up for this?"

"You could call Craig," Jennifer told Meredith. Craig Smythe, student body president and fellow honor student, had been Meredith's date for everything this spring.

But she shook her head. "You guys go." Meredith nodded toward her father's dry cleaning shop on the opposite side of Hazelhurst's main street. "I'll get a ride home with Dad."

"Nothing doing," Sonny said, catching her hand before she could move away. "It'll be more fun with everyone there." Cyndi noticed he coaxed the first real smile of the afternoon from Meredith. He had that talent—of putting everyone at ease.

He turned to Ryder. "Hey, man, you're coming, aren't you?"

Ryder stood to the side, watching them all with his usual, amused little smile. "You want me to?" He paused, his smile fading. "I mean, Sonny-boy, with all your girls along . . ."

Silence fell over the group. Puzzled, Cyndi watched the look—half anger, half surprise—that flashed between the two boys.

Then Jennifer began to laugh, that throaty, bubbly laughter that was so unmistakably hers. And soon they were all laughing. Not because anything funny had happened. But because laughing eased the sudden, odd tension that had seized them all. They laughed because they were eighteen. Because it was a Saturday afternoon in May . . .

And ten years later, Cyndi could still remember that Saturday. In clear, crystallized detail, the day lived in her memory. The last Saturday of her childhood. That Saturday when she was still Sonny's girl.

"Sonny."

She jumped, realizing she had whispered his name out loud. Still caught in the past, she looked around her bedroom, half expecting to hear her friends' laughter.

But the day was just a memory.

That warm, tragic May was dead and buried.

And she hadn't belonged to Sonny for quite some time.

Impatiently she tore the reunion invitation in half. She cursed the chain of events that had revived the past. If she hadn't received the invitation, if she hadn't seen Sonny's challenge in Nick Calderaro's smile...

Calderaro. Cyndi frowned. If ever there was a problem that should force past mistakes from her mind, it should be Nick Calderaro. Besides, apart from the smile, he wasn't at all like Sonny.

Yet she would bet her life he was going to be trouble.

Chapter Three

The room was sun washed, spacious and filled with color—vibrant shades of cinnamon, gold and turquoise. A pleasing room, Nick thought, pausing beside one of its many western-facing windows. Cyndi Saint's entire home was comfortable, unexpectedly warm and welcoming.

In what had become a reflex action this afternoon, he searched the crowded room until he located Cyndi. She was seated across the way, engrossed in conversation with the man who had been hired to direct her new show. Her expression was as earnest as a schoolgirl's. As Nick studied her, he decided he was either getting old or simply losing his ability to read people. For he couldn't get a fix on who Cyndi was.

"How's the wine?"

Without his noticing, Lin Redding had joined Nick beside the window. Blankly he looked first at her and then at the empty wineglass he clutched in his right hand. "It was fine," he said at last.

She grinned and held up a carafe. "I mean, do you want more?"

"Sure." He laughed sheepishly as Lin filled his glass. "You know, this was a good idea—everyone meeting casually to toss around some ideas about the show." Lin, who was clearly relishing her new position as executive producer, had conducted an informal but productive meeting that had now dissolved into a social gathering.

Lin glanced around the room where over a dozen people—writers, assistants and consultants—were clustered in groups, talking. "I was hesitant about asking anyone to give up their Sunday afternoon, but I thought getting away from the office and studio would put us all at ease. Pulling this show together is going to take a lot of work. I want the staff to become a family, to get comfortable with each other."

"I agree."

"So you're pleased?"

"Of course."

Lin seemed relieved. "Good. The way you looked a minute ago, I thought something might be wrong."

"I was just thinking about this room." At Lin's puzzled look, he went on to explain, "This isn't what I expected when you told me we'd meet at Miss Saint's."

"You expected a certain kind of house?"

"All during the drive from the city I kept visualizing one of those trendy, sparsely furnished places. You know, that neotech, minimalist stuff you see decorators do, with chairs that look like torture devices."

Lin's eyes widened.

"You know," Nick explained. "Chrome tubes with leather strips to hold you off the floor."

Rather pointedly, Lin gazed at the plump swallow-you-up couches grouped near the center of the room. "Torture devices aren't Cyndi's style."

"I guess not." Nick glanced from the pillows piled beside the fireplace to the colorful Southwestern-flavored wall hanging above it. "I really like this," he said finally.

"And it's hard for you to admit liking anything about Cyndi, even her house."

Lin's tone was carefully nonaccusatory, and Nick replied in kind. "If what you're trying to get at are my reservations about her hosting the show...well, we've been over that before."

"I believe you're worried because you still don't know Cyndi very well. Her personality is going to *make* this show."

"Really?" Swallowing a sip of wine, Nick used the pause to watch Lin react to his skepticism. "Everyone—especially you, Miss Redding—keeps telling me how warm and personable Cyndi is. I'll admit she comes across well on her exercise show, but in all the meetings we've had during the past two weeks, I haven't seen her do much of anything but listen."

"What do you want her to do?"

"Express an opinion, maybe. Give us her ideas."

"We've got plenty of people with lots of opinions and ideas," Lin retorted. "Cyndi will be ready to do her job when the camera is on."

Nick shrugged. "We'll see, won't we?" Ignoring Lin's now-obvious irritation, he nodded toward Cyndi. "I will say one thing—it's good to see her mingling with everyone on staff. A lot of on-camera talents like to hold themselves apart from the behind-the-scenes people. I've seen that kind of behavior all too often, so I know there's less tension if everyone works together. It was a nice touch for her to volunteer her home today."

"It wasn't a *touch*. As you'll probably discover, Cyndi is just a nice person."

The chastising note in Lin's voice made Nick smile. "'Nice' won't win ratings."

"I don't know about that. Nice has taken her pretty far."

"Are you sure beauty has nothing to do with it?"

Lin shook her head. "Beauty might have gotten her the first job, when a local television station took her from an exercise class she was leading and gave her a segment on their noon news program. But on camera, Cyndi has a special quality. I know her better than most people, and I'm the first to admit she's a little reserved in person. But when the camera's on, there's an eagerness about her, a sense that she's working hard to please. People respond to that. When she smiles, they almost forget she's beautiful."

Not all people, Nick thought as Cyndi stood and bestowed a brilliant smile on her director. The guy appeared momentarily dazzled. No *man* could ever forget she was beautiful. Nick certainly wouldn't, especially if she gave him such a genuine smile.

"Nick?"

He started, realizing his attention had gone back to Cyndi. Too much wine, he decided and set his half-empty glass on the tiled windowsill.

Obviously repeating herself, Lin said, "I'm sorry you still have no faith in Cyndi's abilities. I think she'll surprise you."

"Maybe." Again Nick looked at Cyndi, who had moved across the room to chat with another group.

Beside him, Lin chuckled softly. "Strange, isn't it?"

"Strange?" he repeated, not knowing what she meant.

"You doubt Cyndi's ability to attract and hold an audience, yet you haven't been able to keep your eyes off her all afternoon." Turning on her heel, Lin left Nick trying to come up with a suitable retort.

She had her nerve, he thought. Automatically he reached to loosen a too-tight necktie. Only he wasn't wearing a tie, so instead he grabbed his wineglass and drained its contents. Just because he and Lin had been working so easily together on plans for the show didn't mean she could be impertinent. He was her boss, for God's sake. And so what if he had been watching Cyndi all afternoon? He had been observing how she handled herself, trying to imagine how she would come across as host of the show. How she would...

Oh, come off it, Calderaro. Impatient with the excuses he was giving himself, he headed for the dining alcove and the antique sideboard Cyndi had filled with food. Healthy food. He eyed the raw vegetables, fruits and cheeses with disgust. At the moment, he would prefer something fried and fattening and a beer instead of this California wine.

Putting down his wineglass, he turned and caught Cyndi studying him. She was quick to glance away, but a flush stole into her cheeks.

He shoved his hands into his pockets and watched her—blatantly, uncaring if she or Lin or anyone else in the room noticed. There was nothing wrong with a man looking at a beautiful woman. Surely Cyndi was used to men's stares.

If only he could put her into one of the categories in which he divided women. Her beauty and high-profile career meant he should be able to group her with all the other bitch-goddesses he had encountered in this business. But as he had discovered on their very first meeting, that label didn't quite fit. She was much closer to an ice queen, very cool and composed. And something told him that was just a pose. From the beginning he had seen she was much too... vulnerable. He always came back to that word when he tried to describe Cyndi. And he had been trying to describe her to himself far too often over the past two weeks.

During these preliminary meetings, they had been very polite to each other. Distantly polite. He had waited, thinking at any moment she would reveal an unattractive, demanding side. He almost wanted her to be difficult. If she acted as he expected her to, he might not be so fascinated by her.

And, yes, he was fascinated. He hated admitting it even to himself, but it was the truth. It explained why he was now staring at her like a smitten fool.

With some effort, Nick tore his gaze away. He briefly considered another glass of wine but settled instead on pushing through the swinging door next to the sideboard. He needed distance from the woman, not alcohol. But once in the airy, plant-filled kitchen, he didn't hesitate to rummage through the refrigerator, where he found a beer.

Twisting the cap off the bottle, he leaned against a cabinet. He took a long drink and allowed his thoughts to go back to Cyndi once more. Last week he had decided she had won her new job by bamboozling the entire network with her beauty. Harris was the obvious candidate, but he was the most married man Nick had ever known. Plus, he had admitted his own doubts about Cyndi in the beginning. So Nick had begun looking around, trying to decide which of the other network head honchos Cyndi was sleeping with.

But that theory just didn't wash. It didn't fit the woman whom he had heard calling the network chief "sir."

A door across the kitchen slammed, and Nick looked up as a man came inside. Not appearing to notice Nick, he dropped a gray laundry bag to the floor and went straight for the refrigerator, coming up with a beer. He looked at home in the kitchen, and because he was young, blond and handsome, he appeared to be an appropriate match for Cyndi Saint. And for some reason, that made Nick feel decidedly sour.

"Hello," he said, surprised by the gruff sound of his own greeting.

The younger man turned around quickly, looking startled. By way of explanation, Nick jerked his head toward the living room and held up his beer. "I left the wine out there and came in search of something a little more to my taste."

"Out there?" the other man echoed as he crossed the room. Then a smile broke across his face. "Oh, yeah, I forgot Cyndi was having Lin and some other people over. That explains the cars out front. I thought one of our neighbors was having a party."

Our neighbors. Who was this guy? Nick prepared to find out, but Cyndi's appearance interrupted him. She paused in the doorway. "I didn't expect you home," she said to the younger man.

He caught the door before it could close behind her. "My schedule got changed. And I'm starving. Any party food left?"

Cyndi glanced at Nick. "I take it you two have met?"

"Sort of." Nick held out his hand, introducing himself.

"Devlin Saint." The man's handshake was firm, his smile pleasant. "Cyndi's brother."

Brother. Nick glanced from one to the other, now seeing the resemblance. Devlin nodded to Nick and went into the living room. Someone—Lin, perhaps—called his name. Then the door closed, muffling the conversation and laughter from the other room. Cyndi remained in the kitchen, however, regarding Nick with what he could only describe as a guarded expression. "I saw you come in here. Can I get you something?"

Again he held up his bottle. "I hope you don't mind."

"Of course not."

"My family, being the good Italians that they are, can't understand this preference I have for beer over wine. Back home—"

"Which is where?"

"Boston. Two of my sisters run a bakery down in Little Italy."

"Two of them?"

"There are four in all," Nick explained. "Mary and Donna and the twins, Lucy and Joan. I'm the baby." Cyndi arched an eyebrow at that, and Nick grinned. "There are only five years between Mary, who's the oldest and me, but she's always been good at bossing me around."

Cyndi's expression became even more skeptical. "Are the rest of your sisters still in Boston?"

"Absolutely. With all their husbands and kids. I'm the maverick in the family." He grinned again. "A beer-drinking, globe-trotting bachelor—a source of constant dismay to them all."

Cyndi looked as if she wanted to agree with their dismay. Nick waited, half hoping she'd make some comment and they could spar a little. Anger might make her unbend. But instead, her movements jerky, she merely opened the refrigerator door and peered inside. "I guess other people might have preferred beer, too, but I don't think there's enough...."

As she bent forward, Nick admired the way her hair, as bright as pure, undiluted sunlight, spilled across her cheek. The style was loose today, not scooped back from her face as she usually wore it. The casual style, along with her roomy white sweater and matching leggings made her seem younger. He wondered if she had deliberately downplayed her looks. Then she straightened and closed the refrigerator door, and the sweater's wide neckline slipped, revealing a smooth expanse of shoulder. Nick swallowed hard, thinking looks as spectacular as Cyndi's couldn't be downplayed.

Feeling compelled to defuse the suddenly charged atmosphere, he asked, "So you and Devlin share the house?"

"Sort of. It's my house." She explained that Devlin's schedule kept him at the hospital most of the time.

"I thought he was someone else." At Cyndi's cocked eyebrow, Nick elaborated, "You know—husband, lover, live-in. A woman like you..." He stopped, not sure why he was saying any of this.

But Cyndi wasn't letting him off the hook so easily. "A woman like me? What kind of woman is that?"

"I only meant to say someone so attractive—"

"Do you think attractive women have such a monopoly on husbands, lovers and live-ins?"

Nick shook his head. "Of course not, but I guess I thought you'd have someone."

"Maybe I do."

"So you do, right?"

She almost smiled. "I didn't say that."

He chuckled, a pleasant sound that made Cyndi think there must be a likable person beneath the detached, assessing facade Nick Calderaro had shown her thus far.

He set down his beer and leaned back, his hands braced to either side of him on the edge of the counter. The stance made his casual blue polo shirt stretch across his chest, but it was his smile Cyndi's gaze returned to—the smile that had haunted her for nearly two weeks.

"I like this," he said.

"This?"

"You—not being so...so withdrawn when I'm around."

"I didn't realize that's how I've been."

"Maybe *withdrawn* is the wrong word," he drawled, thinking he would bait her some more. "Maybe *cold* is better."

Cold was a description Cyndi had heard often from men—from Sonny, from her husband, from the man she had almost married last year. Yet repetition had never dulled the sting. Turning from Nick, she opened a drawer and pulled out some napkins, hoping he couldn't see his words had affected her in the least. Silently she counted to ten—exactly as her mother would have told her to do—and she was smiling when she looked up.

But there was something in his expression that told her she hadn't fooled him at all. As he had done since their first meeting, this man saw right through her smile.

Murmuring an excuse about getting back to her guests, Cyndi left him in the kitchen. Throughout the next half hour or so she threw herself into conversation, trying to be warm, trying to be anything but what Nick Calderaro said she was. He watched her. She could feel his regard even as he talked with others, even when he was across the room. By the time people started leaving, she was ready to jump out of her skin.

But too soon, there remained only Devlin and Lin and Nick. A relaxed Nick, who had settled on one end of a couch and appeared ready to stay. Lin looked at him and then at Cyndi, clearly unsure about whether to stay or go.

Devlin seemed oblivious to any out-of-the-ordinary vibrations. "I'm sorry, folks, but I have to go get something more substantial than carrot sticks and broccoli dip, and having looked in my sister's fridge, I know I won't find it here. Anybody else feel like burritos? Lin?"

Lin's dark hair gleamed in the fading sunlight as she shook her head. "I thought I'd just stick around here." Uncertainly she glanced from Cyndi to Nick to her watch. "I've got plans later on, but—"

Devlin cut in, teasingly, "Another date with *that* guy, Lin?" For several weeks, Lin had been seeing someone new, someone Cyndi hadn't met. Lin had been less than forthcoming about him, but Cyndi wasn't going to pry into her friend's business unless invited to do so.

Her brother had no such restraint. "Who is this mystery guy anyway?"

"Devlin," Cyndi said quickly. "I thought you were hungry."

"So I am." Devlin caught Lin's arm and started toward the kitchen. "Come on, you can walk me to my car and tell me all the details."

Though Lin resisted, it was only a matter of minutes before she had collected her purse and briefcase and disappeared with a fast-talking Devlin.

And Cyndi was left alone with Nick.

Her cat, obviously thinking everyone was gone, strolled in from the bedrooms, took one look at Nick and left again.

He chuckled. "Editorial opinion?"

"Lolita hates all strangers," Cyndi explained.

"Lolita?"

"She's precocious."

Again Nick laughed, but instead of relaxing Cyndi, the sound made her more nervous than ever. The man looked as if he could stay all night. Brightly she said, "Can I get you something else to drink? I think there's another beer. Or maybe some coffee?"

"Nothing, thanks."

"Are you sure?"

"Positive." In a movement that was all masculine grace, he flexed his shoulders. "I have to tell you, this is a truly comfortable couch." He settled even deeper into the cushions. Cyndi couldn't stop her frown, and he asked, "I'm not keeping you from anything, am I?"

He had given her a good excuse for getting rid of him, but Cyndi didn't take him up on it. She knew he would somehow be able to tell she was lying. Just as she was certain any kind of personal conversation with him would reveal all sorts of secrets she preferred to keep hidden.

So she schooled her features into her unfaltering smile and perched on the edge of the couch across from the one he occupied. "The meeting went well, didn't it?"

He nodded but said nothing.

For several minutes she rattled on about the show and its staff. Nick was silent, watching her. Nervously Cyndi smoothed her hair back from her face, searching for something, anything that would get a response from him.

"Why are you doing all of this?" he asked finally.

The question startled her. "Doing what?"

"The smile. The flip of the hair. The beauty queen routine."

"I don't know what you're talking about."

"Yeah, you do." He sat forward, his posture as casual as his tone. "A little while ago, in the kitchen, you were real. You had dropped that fake, cold..."

That word again. She didn't want to hear this. Cyndi stood, trying to be as pleasant as she could. "Listen, I don't know what you want from me—"

"I want you to stop playing games."

"I'm not—"

"Yes, you are," he cut in, his voice becoming harsher. "For the last few minutes you've been playing entertain-the-boss. But that's not what I'm interested in. I stuck around here because I thought maybe, at last, I was going to see the real you, the woman with the comfortable couch, the brother and the cat, the person everybody tells me is so special."

Cyndi tossed her head. "It's very clear you don't think I'm special. You don't even like me."

"As Lin pointed out to me a little while ago—I don't even know you." Nick got up from the couch and stepped closer, close enough for her to see the fine lines fanning out from the corners of his eyes, close enough that she caught the faint, spicy scent of his after-shave.

"Do you have to know me?" she asked when his scrutiny of her had gone on a moment too long for comfort.

"No, I guess I don't have to."

But he wanted to. Those unspoken words hung between them, as if suspended from some invisible thread. They made Cyndi's heart pound hard against her chest.

"Just who are you?" Nick muttered. "Who is Cyndi Saint? Do you know the answer yourself?"

The question was unsettling, not just because this hard, demanding man asked it, but because Cyndi had asked it so often of herself. Knowing who she was and what she wanted might mean she'd stop stumbling through life, stop going from one accident to another. But how did one find the answer?

Nick's next question cut into her thoughts. "I guess women like you never really know themselves, do they?"

Cyndi blinked. "Women like me?"

"You know, women with titles in their past— homecoming queens, flower-festival queens. You were the queen of something back where you came from, weren't you?"

His assumptions made her angry. "You're hung up on that, aren't you?"

"What do you mean?"

"Attractive women. You keep generalizing about them. Do you dislike us as a matter of principle or is it something personal?"

His dark eyes narrowed, telling her she'd struck a sore spot. "I've been in television since I was eighteen, almost twenty years, and I've seen a few too many women of your type get ahead just because they have pretty forms and plastic smiles."

"My type?"

"Yeah, *Queenie,* your type. With your kind of face." Nick touched her cheek with his fingers.

And felt her all the way to his bones.

No matter what he told himself or her or everyone else, he knew she wasn't just a type. Her vulnerability—no, he couldn't get away from that word—was as clear as her brilliant blue eyes. She was warm and real, as real as the desire slamming through his body, as tangible as the need to lower his mouth to hers.

He almost followed that crazy impulse. For one heavy, potent moment, they stood poised on the brink of a kiss. But Nick caught himself before he fell into that abyss. He drew his fingers from her soft cheek. Dragging his gaze from her full, kissable lips took more effort.

"I have plans," Cyndi said abruptly, her voice unsteady.

Her words took a few seconds to seep into his befuddled brain. "Plans?"

"You . . . you asked before if you were keeping me from something." The muscles in her throat worked as she swallowed. "I just remembered I do have plans. So if you'll pardon me . . ."

The lie was as transparent as they came, but it was the sweet, ladylike way in which Cyndi told it that made Nick grin. "If you want me to get the hell out of here, just tell me, Queenie."

"I wish you wouldn't call me that."

"Then stop acting like Queen of the Daisy Festival and be straight with me. If you want something, say it."

Bright flags of color bloomed in her cheeks. "Please go."

The polite request amused him. "Please?"

"All right!" she snapped. "I want you to go. Now."

"That's more like it."

Shoulders squared, Cyndi marched across the room. "Let me show you to the door."

Moments later, he paused on the threshold, just long enough to toss her an irreverent grin and an equally cocky, "See you at the studio, Queenie."

Queenie.

Princess.

The despised nicknames—one so immediate, the other a memory—seemed to merge in Cyndi's mind as she slammed her front door. She knew she shouldn't have given in to her angry impulse; her mother never would have. But the only thing she regretted was the door hadn't closed on Nick Calderaro's neck.

* * *

The studio where Cyndi's new show was being taped wasn't too large. But she thought the set designers had made judicious use of the space by devising three sections that roughly paralleled the show's format.

The central area was a mix of warm colors, earthenware pottery and comfortable furniture, a relaxed setting that reminded Cyndi of her own living room. The couches and chairs could be arranged in various configurations, depending on the number of guests and the program topic.

To one side of this set was a small but fully equipped kitchen. The show had a nutritionist who would be featured often, but Cyndi would also be asked to join cookbook authors and other guest chefs in whipping up health-conscious dishes.

Opposite the kitchen was a workout area where Cyndi would tape most of her exercise segments and talk with whatever fitness experts happened to be guests.

The show had been titled *A Better You.* Cyndi thought it an appropriate name since their focus would be on looking better, feeling healthier and living a good life. In addition to herself and the nutritionist, a doctor was scheduled to do a daily health digest dealing chiefly with the concerns of women. A feature reporter would present stories with a business slant, again with an eye to what interested women most.

Each hour-long show would be taped segment by segment and then edited together, hopefully achieving a seamless, up-tempo flow. Though the sets and topics might seem familiar, the program wouldn't look like every other talk show. Lin called the format a video magazine, with fast cuts and snappy graphics. There had been some talk of a studio audience for the interview and workout segments Cyndi would handle. But there wasn't room in their current studio. Cyndi had heard Nick and Lin discussing the possibility of moving to a larger studio at some point in the future. The thought of working in front of an audience scared Cyndi to death.

As if she wasn't frightened enough already.

They had been in preproduction only a month— readying the set, coming up with story ideas, scheduling guests. Nick and Harris wanted the show off the ground in mid-March, only five weeks away. It was time to start getting stories in the can. So today Cyndi would tape her first segment with a personal trainer who worked with some of Hollywood's newest and brightest stars. As planned, the segment wouldn't be too different from what Cyndi had been doing on her exercise program for the past two years, but during all that time, Nick Calderaro hadn't been watching from the sidelines.

He would today.

Barely a half hour before she was due on the set, Cyndi faced herself in the mirror that spanned one wall of her dressing-room/office. She adjusted the strap on her neon-pink leotard and tried to tell herself Nick's presence wouldn't matter. She could do this job and do it well.

Behind her, Lin smiled her reassurance. "You look sensational."

"As our favorite network executive would say, 'Looking good ain't the problem.'"

"Nick's really been getting to you, hasn't he?"

Cyndi turned to face Lin. "Doesn't he get to you? He's always hanging around, making suggestions, watching all the run-throughs we've done, calling attention to everyone's shortcomings."

Softly Lin said, "I think that's part of his job."

"Well, I don't like it." Nervous energy joined with her irritation as Cyndi stalked to the desk and shuffled through the notes for the upcoming taping. "Lin, you're the executive producer, the show's *only* producer. I think if something is good enough for you, Nick Calderaro should be satisfied. I mean, don't you wish he would leave us alone? Don't you resent his interference?"

Lin's silence was telling. Cyndi looked at her in surprise. "Are you beginning to like the man?"

"Liking him has nothing to do with it." Lin sighed and pushed a hand through her dark hair. "The fact of the matter is, he's good at what he does."

"So are you."

"But this is the first time I've been a producer."

"That doesn't mean Nick's suggestions are always right."

"Of course not. I've disagreed with some of his ideas, and we've had to compromise a few times. But I'd be acting like a prima donna if I didn't listen to what he has to say."

Ashamed to realize she was behaving like something of a prima donna herself, Cyndi tossed her notes aside and went back to the mirror.

"Come on, Cyndi," Lin coaxed. "Even you have to admit the man has had some terrific ideas."

"Even me?" Cyndi grabbed a bottle and blasted her French-braided hair with an unnecessary coat of hair spray. "I guess that means since I know so little about what I'm doing, it must be hard for me to recognize someone who is an expert."

Lin let loose with one of her best expletives. "I'm not even going to try to reason with you. You're about to tape the first segment. You're understandably nervous. You've been working too hard—"

"Nick says I don't work hard enough."

"Oh, Cyndi, don't take the man so seriously. He's just pushing you to do your best. I do the same thing. So does Joe," Lin added, naming the show's eager, young director.

"But you and Joe don't..." Feeling frustrated, Cyndi closed her eyes. Getting all hot and bothered about Nick just before she had to go on was not a good idea. "Never mind," she murmured, and forced herself to draw several deep breaths.

But Lin didn't let it drop. "Joe and I don't what?"

Gritting her teeth, Cyndi thought of the fantasy that had taken hold of her during the past few, frustrating weeks with Nick. "You and Joe," she said, precisely enunciating each word, "don't make me want to put you both in body casts. Nick does."

Lin's laughter filled the tiny room. "Goodness, Cyndi, I never knew you had such a violent streak."

Cyndi relaxed enough to smile. "I never have before. But there's something about that man..."

"Sparks do go off when you two are together."

The teasing note in Lin's voice made Cyndi glance at her. "What do you mean, sparks?"

With elaborate casualness, Lin straightened the sleeve of her red silk jacket. "I'm just saying that there's something distinctly sexual in the air when you and Nick are in the same room."

"Sexual?" The word was a croak, forced through Cyndi's dry throat. Sex had nothing to do with her reactions to Nick. So what if they had almost kissed a few weeks ago at her house? It didn't matter that every time they saw each other he watched her like a tomcat on the prowl. That wasn't sexual. That was... was... what? She wasn't sure. She didn't want to know.

"Don't look so shocked," Lin said, grinning as she turned toward the door. "Devlin was the first one who noticed a little fizz between the two of you."

"Devlin?" Cyndi repeated. "Why would he—"

"Remember? At your house after the meeting, Devlin practically threw me out of the house so you and Nick could be alone."

"My brother, the optimist. You'd think with my matrimonial and romantic record he'd give up. And Nick is certainly not a likely candidate."

Lin laughed. "Well, you could be forgiven if you found the man fascinating. He is one of those dark, dangerous types."

"I don't go for those types."

"Maybe you should."

"Oh, yeah, sure."

"I'm not kidding. Men who aren't safe aren't so bad." Lin's smile faded. "Sometimes."

Cyndi frowned, not sure what her friend meant.

Pausing with her hand on the doorknob, Lin explained, "Lately, I've begun to think we spend too much time worrying about who *seems* to be right or wrong for us."

"Us?"

Lin's smile was sheepish. "I guess I'm really just talking about myself."

"Problems with the new guy?" The question popped out before Cyndi thought. "I'm sorry, Lin. I didn't mean to ask that. I know everyone is driving you crazy by asking when they're going to meet Jacob."

"No, no, it's okay," Lin said, her expression growing thoughtful. "In fact, I've been wondering why you haven't asked about him."

"Well, we've been so busy we haven't had a chance to talk." Cyndi hesitated, then went on, "And I didn't want to pry, either, Lin."

Shaking her head, Lin leaned against the door. "Honestly, Cyndi, sometimes you really amaze me. Why would you ever think you'd be prying by asking me a question? We're friends."

Cyndi wasn't sure how to answer Lin. Not prying, not getting too personal, were lessons her mother had taught her. But not until this moment had she realized she was still applying those rules to her relationship with Lin. She didn't want to hold Lin at arm's length, just as she had done Meredith and Jennifer and every other person who might have grown close to her.

"I'm sorry," Cyndi told Lin, feeling genuinely contrite. "I guess I've been too immersed in the show.

You and I haven't really had time to talk. But I want to meet Jacob," she added quickly. "Soon. You act as if he's different, like he's..."

"Special," Lin completed for her. "Jacob's really special." She frowned, a gesture that belied the breathless note in her voice. "Maybe that's why I haven't brought him around yet. Or told you about him. Or...oh, gosh, Cyndi, I just don't—"

A knock on the door interrupted Lin. She was needed in the studio, so there wasn't time for them to talk further. Cyndi was left alone to wonder about this man who had so unsettled her intrepid friend. She had never seen Lin like this—all fluttery and uncertain, not at all like her usual self.

"Or at least not like the *self* I know," Cyndi murmured. It was strange to think she might not know Lin as well as she had imagined. Just as she hadn't known Meredith or Jennifer. Impatiently she gathered her notes again, wondering why she thought of her childhood friends so often these days. Since receiving that reunion notice, she had expended too much energy on worry over the past. It was useless. She couldn't change what had happened. She couldn't alter the fact that she and those two girls hadn't really been friends at all. It hadn't been their fault; they probably tried to reach her. It had been her problem. She had pushed them away.

Then, when she needed them, on that morning after the prom when her perfectly planned little world had been destroyed...

"No," Cyndi told herself, standing up and starting for the door. "I'm not going to go over this again. I'm not eighteen. I'm an adult. What's past is past." Chin high, she strode out of her office and down the hall to the studio, where the activity level was too high to allow her to think of anything but the job she had to do.

The welcome she received there was gratifying. Lin and Harris Fielding, who were in a huddle near the door, sent her encouraging smiles. Joe and his assistant beamed at her. The makeup artist, gushing over how wonderful she looked, pulled her to the side for a quick touch-up. Camera operators, sound technicians and all the others she had gotten to know from her other show or in the past weeks called out greetings.

Only Nick said nothing.

Standing to the side, arms folded across his chest, he watched Cyndi move through the studio. There was much to admire in what her slender curves did for her tights and leotard. More admirable, however, was the way everyone reacted to her. She was liked. As she responded to the warm hello of her guest for this segment, Nick wondered why her popularity surprised him.

For weeks, he had seen the way she dealt with colleagues. Yes, as Lin had told him, she was reserved, maybe even a little shy. But she treated others with respect. They gave the same back to her. During all the run-throughs he had insisted Lin and Joe do, Cyndi hadn't whined or complained or become impatient. Even though she was still taping her regular exercise show, as well as preparing a workout videotape, she had made herself available for every production meeting.

Nick had pushed her, just as he had promised her he would. After each practice session, he had reviewed the tapes with the staff and added his critique to Lin and Joe's. Cyndi had taken his suggestions with outward calm. And on the next run-through she did everything she could to improve. In short, she worked damn hard. He often had the feeling that she was doing her best to show him something.

Now she chatted easily with her guest while the lighting and sound personnel made a few last-minute adjustments. Joe gave everyone some instructions, and quiet was called on the set. As the countdown toward taping began, Cyndi put her smile in place.

And briefly she glanced at Nick. Unable to stop himself, he grinned, and her perfect little chin rose. When she was given the signal to begin, there was an extra lift in her voice as she addressed the camera. Her intro to the segment was faultless. Unfortunately, the sound mixer wasn't satisfied with what he was hearing. Joe had to cut the action, and they had to begin again.

And again.

Five times Cyndi offered the same opening patter.

Five times she was just right, while everyone else was wrong.

With a grace and patience that contrasted with the restlessness of her guest and the crew, she waited until a problem with her cordless microphone was corrected. Then she completed the segment.

Like a pro.

When it was over, Nick remained where he was while everyone congratulated each other on a job well done. Though he said little, he felt absurdly proud.

Harris edged over to his side, a smile crinkling his sad eyes. "Still worried, my friend?"

"She did good," Nick admitted. "But then, she's done this kind of thing before."

"Damn, but you're hard-hearted, Nick. This was the first thing she's done for this show. It had to have felt different. You ought to tell her she did a good job."

"And give her a reason to stop trying so hard?" Chuckling, Nick shook his head.

Harris rolled his eyes heavenward but said nothing more about Cyndi as they left the studio and made their way to a meeting.

Throughout the long afternoon, Nick did his best to concentrate on plans for another new program, but Cyndi kept intruding on his thoughts. Had she expected him to congratulate her on how well the taping had gone? On his way out, he had told Lin and Joe he was pleased, but he hadn't even glanced at Cyndi. It wasn't his way to go on and on with compliments. When a task was satisfactorily completed, he usually gave everyone a nod and started preparing for the next part of the job. Cyndi still had a long way to go before she had proved herself satisfactory at this job, and one good segment didn't make the program. But he could have said something today. It was a courtesy he would give anyone. And just because this particular woman had gotten under his skin . . .

Yes, dammit, the woman got to him. But that wasn't her fault. He couldn't let an attraction interfere with a professional relationship. Past mistakes had taught him that lesson.

But the way he had treated Cyndi was still bothering Nick when he got on the elevator that evening. It was after eight, and the building was almost deserted. Certainly he couldn't expect anyone to still be on *A Better You*'s set. But he punched the button for that floor, anyway. And though he told himself he was wasting his time, he strolled down the hall to Cyndi's dressing room. The door was ajar, but Nick didn't go inside.

He stood in the hall, listening, as over and over, Cyndi rehearsed the intro for the interview she was scheduled to tape tomorrow afternoon. She varied her inflection. She groaned. She told herself not to screw up. And there was an earnestness in her voice that touched Nick. The heart his friend had said was hard was softening when he finally pushed the door open.

Looking startled, Cyndi turned in her chair in front of her mirror. "Nick," she whispered.

Until then, he hadn't realized she'd never called him by his first name. And something in that one husky word subtly but surely altered the atmosphere in the small room. Nick took a deep breath, then realized his mistake when all he smelled was Cyndi. The air was filled with the scent he had unconsciously memorized the first time they met. And right now that fragrance made him think of crushed roses and rumpled sheets. It was a dangerously vivid image.

Cyndi stood, repeating his name.

Nick dragged his mind from the dead-end street he had started down. He forced himself to relax, to grin, to say, "Well, Queenie, I guess you might do okay, after all."

Chapter Four

Watching catsup ooze onto a mound of salted, greased French fries, Cyndi murmured, "I don't know how you talked me into this, Nick."

"You mean dinner?"

She eyed his cheeseburger—the biggest, with-everything burger she had ever seen—and shuddered. "This isn't dinner. This is a cholesterol feeding frenzy."

Nick chuckled and rolled up the sleeves of his white shirt, obviously prepared to enjoy his meal. "Hey, don't complain. You got your salad, didn't you?"

The salad in question consisted of a few lettuce leaves and tomatoes piled high with boiled eggs, ham, cheese, turkey and bacon bits. Real bacon. The kind with the fat cooked to a fine crackle. Even without the thick calorie-laden dressing Cyndi had requested on the side, it wasn't her usual kind of salad.

"I'm sorry they didn't have bean sprouts," Nick said.

"I'm sure they've never heard of them." Cyndi darted a glance around the neon-lit diner. With its green-and-gray-checked linoleum floor and gum-chewing waitress, this restaurant in the wrong part of the city seemed a million miles from the Los Angeles-area eateries she knew. When Nick had appeared at her door with his unexpected compliment about the day's work and his even more surprising invitation to dinner, she had imagined something very different. Someplace trendy, perhaps. Never this.

Of course, no one had forced her to come with him. She could have told him no. She could have greeted his cocky grin and his use of that annoying nickname with a cool, polite refusal. But politeness had been the last thing on her mind when she had turned and found him watching her. She had responded to the warmth in his gaze, and somehow, she had wound up in his car.

At first, she had told herself this dinner was in the interest of bringing harmony to their working relationship. But that admirable thought had been replaced by the memory of what Lin had said about sexual sparks. Was sex really what pulled her toward Nick? Was sex the reason she was sitting here wondering how his beard-shadowed cheek would feel to her touch?

Sex. It wasn't a subject Cyndi was comfortable with. Especially with a man like Nick seated mere inches away.

Wishing she'd had the good sense to go home on time, she dug into her salad. She paused before taking a bite, daunted by thoughts of the formfitting leotard she had to wear tomorrow morning. Even with exercise, she had to watch what she ate. The camera added pounds. She decided to eat a little, just enough to quiet her rumbling stomach. But unfortunately, that consideration melted as soon as she bit into an extra crispy slice of bacon.

From behind his king-size burger, Nick grinned at her. "Pretty good, huh?"

"Disgustingly so," she admitted, spearing another fattening forkful. "Tell me again how you found this place."

"Luck," he retorted. "One night, a few years ago when I first moved out here, I was driving around, missing New York—"

"Do you regularly go out driving on strange streets on this side of L.A.?"

"Not regularly, no, but this night, I couldn't sleep. I was missing the noise, you know, the gritty kind of feeling you only find back home."

"I thought Boston was home."

"Just till I was eighteen. That's when I moved to New York, started college and got into television."

"Sounds like a big year."

He shrugged. "I knew what I wanted."

She could imagine that. She knew instinctively he was the kind of person who always knew where he was heading. No accidents in Nick Calderaro's life. "How does an eighteen-year-old get into television?"

"My first job was sweeping floors at an independent station. Then I went over to a network affiliate to run errands. I stayed out of the way most of the time, just soaking in the atmosphere. You can learn a lot by fading into the background and listening."

Cyndi chuckled.

"What's wrong?"

Impulsively she said what she thought, "I just can't imagine you fading into any background."

Grasping his half-empty beer mug, he leaned back, sprawling negligently in the booth's bench, looking very relaxed with his tie loosened and top button undone. Amusement deepened the creases beside his dark eyes as he studied her. "That sounded almost like a compliment, Miss Saint."

She pretended great interest in a water ring on the scarred green tabletop. "Maybe."

"So maybe we don't hate everything about each other?"

She looked up quickly, just long enough to be caught again by his gaze. "I guess we don't. And I think that's good."

"Me, too," he returned. "I like to get along with the people I work with."

"Really?" Cyndi set her fork aside and folded her hands on the table, regarding him with a serious expression. "Then why are you so rotten to me?"

He had the audacity to laugh.

"What is so funny?"

Leaning forward, he trailed a finger across her knuckles. Cyndi did her best not to react to his touch. She didn't flinch, but her entire body tightened.

"You look so prim," Nick murmured. "Like the very best little girl in school."

The description couldn't have fit more perfectly. For Cyndi had once been that very best little girl. She had worn color-coordinated clothes with matching barrettes in her blond curls. She had done her homework. She had stayed clean and neat. She had been polite to her elders. For years and years she had done everything she was supposed to do, everything that would please first her parents and then Sonny and then her husband and everyone else. Perhaps that was what she was still doing.

Nick watched the sadness steal into Cyndi's face and regretted his teasing words. "Hey," he murmured as his hand touched hers. "Something wrong?"

Pulling away, she shook her head. Outside the window beside their booth, the diner's flashing neon sign blinked on and off. The colors changed from red to blue and back again, staining Cyndi's cheek, reflecting in the hammered gold of her tiered earrings. For the first time Nick saw how tired she was. She still looked beautiful, especially in the clingy short skirt and oversize pink jacket she had changed into back at the studio, but she was undeniably weary. Not hard to understand if he considered the pace she had been keeping the past few weeks.

"I'm sorry." His sudden statement made Cyndi's eyes widen, but it couldn't have surprised her more than it did himself. "For being rotten," he went on to explain. "Or making you think I was rotten, anyway."

"An apology, Mr. Calderaro? I'm shocked."

"No, really," Nick insisted, "I'm sorry. Sometimes I forget what it was like."

"What what was like?"

"Being new at this game." He smiled. "I have to stretch my memory a little to remember it, but I think I used to practice in front of the mirror, too."

"I didn't know anyone was listening," Cyndi retorted, flushing. "And besides, tomorrow's interview is important."

The actress scheduled for tomorrow afternoon was a big star whose new book on beauty and fitness would be released about the time the show debuted. She also had a reputation as a temperamental interviewee. Nick had been wondering if Cyndi would be able to handle her, but he knew his doubts were the last thing Cyndi needed tonight. He had heard the nerves in her voice back in her dressing room. The thing to do was shore up her confidence.

"You'll do fine," he said with more conviction than he felt.

Cyndi regarded him with suspicion. "Think so?"

"Listen," he said, settling back in the booth again. "Tomorrow will be a piece of cake."

"I wish I were sure of that."

"Trust me, Cyndi. I was once a reporter, you know. Half the secret of a successful interview is being prepared. And I'd say you're ready."

"Were you always prepared?"

"Of course not." He grinned and drained the last of his beer. "I've got plenty of interview horror stories."

She looked pleased by his admission of a weakness. "Tell me."

"There are too many stories to mention in one night. But one of my worst screwups was when I showed up an hour late to interview a future president."

"Where were you?"

"In a hotel room with an aching head. The press party the night before got a little...umm...out of hand."

She leaned forward. "Did you get the interview anyway?"

"Nope. I got fired."

"How terrible."

He shrugged. "No big deal, Cyndi. I probably had it coming since I was already bored with the job. I looked on my abrupt departure as an opportunity. In three weeks I was an associate producer at another network. It wasn't the only time I lost a job."

"Were you that happy every time you were fired?"

"Hardly." Nick could remember one firing in particular, the one that had proved to him what most of the women in this business were like. That loss had stung, perhaps because it was double-edged. He stared out the window for a moment, reliving the painful lesson, before he turned back to Cyndi. "You need to remember that television—broadcasting, in general—is full of people who have been fired over and over again. It's like a war decoration, a badge of honor."

She sighed deeply. "I have no badges. I don't want any, either."

He wanted to reassure her, but the only advice that came to mind was hardly original. "Just do your best."

She wasn't buying the cliché, either. "Once upon a time I thought my best would be good enough. I've known better for a long time now."

Again sadness settled over her, slumping her shoulders, pulling at the corners of her pretty mouth. More bothered by her distress than he knew was good for him, Nick covered her hand with his once more. This time she didn't pull away.

"Don't worry." He smiled teasingly. "If the ratings on the show don't come through, all they'll do is shoot you."

Though she laughed, he believed her reply. "I'd rather be shot than let everyone down."

"Which is probably why everyone thinks you're so special."

She looked away. "That's silly—"

"You've got quite a cheering section," he insisted. "Harris, Joe, Lin—"

"She's a good friend."

"Even for a friend, she's intensely loyal. Intense about everything."

"Lin's determined," Cyndi agreed. "But I guess that's understandable considering her background."

"Her background?"

She hesitated only slightly before explaining, "Lin and her mother joined her father over here when Lin was ten. The move from Vietnam to a little Nebraska farming community was quite a jump. Added to that was her father's family. They never accepted Lin or her mother, just as her mother's family had rejected them over there."

Nick drew his own conclusion. "So Lin's always been something of an outsider."

"And outsiders often try harder than anyone else."

He studied the all-American pretty face across from him. "You can't know much about being an outsider."

"I know Lin."

"Yes, but what I'm wondering is what makes *you* try so hard. You're not really like Lin, so what is it that drives *you?*"

Fine tendrils of blond hair broke free at Cyndi's temples as she shook her head. "There's nothing—"

"Oh, but there has to be." He tightened his fingers around hers. "We all have an agenda we're trying to fulfill. What's yours? Money? Fame?" Her denial was emphatic. "Then what?" he challenged. "What are you trying to be, Cyndi?"

Her gaze steady on his, she hesitated, then spoke, her voice soft. "I guess I'm still trying to be that very best little girl in school."

"You guess?"

She shifted in her seat, a line of irritation marring the smooth skin of her forehead. "We're all trying to be the best, aren't we?"

"But what does being the best really mean to you?"

"The best is just the best," she retorted. "It means being a success, having people approve of what you do, being happy."

He wondered if she understood how much she had revealed about herself with that simple statement.

"You're saying approval is the same as happiness, aren't you?"

"Obviously you don't think so."

He shrugged. "The approval of other people doesn't rank real high with me."

"Then I don't know what you're doing in television. Pleasing people is all we do."

"First, I please myself."

"Which might explain some of those times you lost your job," Cyndi pointed out, her smile robbing the words of sharpness.

Nick grinned back. "You're probably right. But I don't see the medium only in terms of ratings points."

"That could come as a surprise to the people who hired you as a programming executive."

"Harris knows me," Nick said. "He knows I have a particular vision about good television. Right now I have an opportunity to make the vision a reality. And if that translates into ratings points..." Again he shrugged. "If it doesn't, I'll move on."

Cyndi studied him silently for a moment. "It must be nice to have your kind of attitude."

"It's who I am. Just like my pop, I'm only trying to fight a good fight." He laughed and at Cyndi's puzzled look, explained, "It's a family joke. Pop was a boxer."

"A pro?"

"You could say that. He wasn't the most successful guy who ever stepped into the ring. He was past his prime but still fighting when I was born. He had a tough time feeding five kids, though."

"It must have been hard on your mother."

"Oh, Mama never lost hope. When he won, she rejoiced with him. When he lost, all she would say was 'Tony, did you fight a good fight?' That's what mattered to her." Nick chuckled. "And later on, when Pop was running a gym for other boxers, that's how she greeted him when he came home. In our family it meant you had tried. And even if you failed, fighting a good fight meant you succeeded."

Softly Cyndi said, "It sounds as if you have wonderful parents."

"Had," Nick corrected. "They're both gone." For a moment the loss of those two special people ached inside him anew. Then Cyndi squeezed his hand, the the ache subsided, replaced by an unexpected warmth. He stared at their joined hands, somewhat astounded by the feelings rushing through him. Glancing up, he found the same astonishment in Cyndi's eyes.

They both jerked their hands away at the same time.

He grabbed the first topic of conversation that came to mind. "What about your parents? I guess they're proud of their daughter the television personality."

"Dad seems to take it in stride."

"And your mother?"

Cyndi's eyelashes swept down, shuttering her expression from him. "Mother died suddenly a few years back. The only things she ever saw were the segments I did for the local news here in Los Angeles."

"And she wasn't impressed?"

"It wasn't..." Cyndi paused, biting her lip. Finally she looked up at Nick. "I didn't turn out quite the way Mother expected."

"What did she expect?"

She sighed and glanced out the window. "Let's just say fighting a good fight wasn't enough for her."

Her pain was easy to read, and it left Nick wondering about any woman who wouldn't be pleased by the mere existence of a daughter as lovely as Cyndi.

And she was lovely. Not merely beautiful, but sweet and intelligent. Smarter than he had given her credit for being in the beginning. There was depth to this woman. Layers and layers of complex woman beneath the gorgeous exterior. It would take a man with patience to get to the core of who she was. Nick's patience had never won him any awards, but Cyndi made him think the prize might be worth the effort.

"You folks gonna want something else?"

The waitress's inquiry forced Nick to reluctantly transfer his attention from Cyndi to his watch. "It's late," he murmured.

Cyndi nodded. "And I have a drive home."

"I'll take you."

"No, you won't. My car's back at the studio."

"But I—"

"Excuse me," the waitress interrupted. "But I'm still here. You want some dessert, or what?"

Nick and Cyndi began to laugh, and the waitress, shaking her head, left them a check and walked away.

A silly sort of mood enveloped them during the drive back to the studio. Cyndi spent the time laughing at Nick's stories about the outrageous rock group for whom he had directed several videos last year. It seemed there was no challenge he wouldn't accept. She admired and envied that quality about him. And admiring Nick Calderaro had been the last thing on her mind just hours ago. So perhaps the dinner had injected some harmony into their relationship, after all.

She tried not to think of the warmth of his strong hands holding hers. Or of the tenderness in his voice when he had spoken of his parents. Those things made Nick an even more attractive man. And she didn't want to be attracted to him. It wouldn't go anywhere. In the end, they would just disappoint each other.

But when he turned into the studio's parking lot, she couldn't stop herself wishing they could drive on through the night. She could imagine the drive up the Coast, with this low-slung black Porsche hugging the road like a sleek, deadly cobra.

"Your car surprises me," she said as he drove up the ramp to her parking level.

"You don't like it?"

"Of course. But it seems so California, or something."

"And I'm not California?"

"You told me you miss New York."

He looked at her, smile flashing even in the dim interior of the car. "Maybe I'm missing it less and less, Cyndi. Less and less."

The words were suggestive, but they shouldn't have made her shiver. And when his car pulled alongside hers, she shouldn't have been so reluctant to get out. If she had opened the door right away, Nick might not have touched her cheek. She wouldn't have known the quick, melting moments of desire. The very air between them heated. And, as usual, the panic started inside Cyndi.

Jerking away from his touch, she fumbled for the door handle. "Good…good night, Nick. Thanks for dinner."

"Cyndi?" His hand closed on her elbow.

She was forced to look at him. His eyes were dark, questioning. She was torn between wanting to give him answers and running away. She chose her normal course of action and got out of the car.

Nick came around, took her keys and opened her car door for her, but Cyndi didn't meet his gaze again as she started the engine. He said nothing. He just stood, watching her drive away. She knew he was still standing there when she turned the curve and headed down the ramp and out into the balmy February night.

She gripped the steering wheel, damning the man she had left behind. She didn't need this man in her life. He would make demands. Demands she'd never satisfy. Hadn't she proven that one too many times?

With the wind blowing warm against her cheeks, she headed for the freeway and the hour commute home. But it wasn't the lights of Los Angeles that winked and passed like a blur outside her car. It wasn't only Nick that she ran from. For there had been another night like this—warm, with just a hint of coolness.

Prom night.

Ten years ago.

The night she had started running…

Clutching her seat belt strap, Cyndi watched the lavender shadows of the May evening slip past her window with gathering speed. "Sonny, please slow down."

Though his mouth tightened, Sonny obediently eased up on the gas pedal. "That better?"

"I just don't want you to get another ticket. Don't you remember what your father said?"

"Yeah, yeah." Pausing at a stop sign, Sonny raked a hand through his blond hair. "Between you and my old man, there's not a chance in hell I'll do anything wrong."

"What is it you want to do?"

His cocked eyebrow and grin supplied a multitude of answers, and flushing, Cyndi turned away. Muttering something she couldn't catch, Sonny turned up the volume on the radio.

Cyndi started to protest, but then closed her mouth. She didn't want to argue. During the past week, Sonny had done nothing but harp at her, but tonight had been different. They'd had a nice dinner at the best restaurant in Hazelhurst. They were going to have a great time at the dance. The after-prom party the senior class parents always gave would follow. Cyndi had permission from her parents to stay out until morning if she wanted. Tonight—every minute of it— was the night she would remember for the rest of her life.

Tonight.

The word settled like a heavy stone in Cyndi's stomach.

With nervous fingers, she touched the bright nosegay in her lap. The flowers were deep rose, white and the palest of pinks, all edged in lace, with ribbons in the same shades cascading from the handle. It was a beautiful bouquet, exactly what she had wanted. Her mother had ordered it, so Sonny wouldn't have to. Cyndi thought she would have settled for something less spectacular if Sonny had chosen it himself.

But the flowers weren't important. What mattered was the way Sonny had looked at her when he first saw her in her dress. Tall and broad shouldered in his black tux, he had stood in the foyer of her house, watching her come down the stairs. His eyes, more green than blue tonight, had shone. He had taken her hand and called her "Princess" in the sweetest, most special way. He was acting like the Sonny she had known and loved all her life. Sonny would make tonight what she needed it to be. He would take care of everything.

She turned to study his handsome, familiar profile. He had always been there for her. During her first, terrifying days of school. At the junior high hop when she was certain she would look silly on the dance floor. And that same year on a hot July Fourth, with fireworks exploding over The Green downtown, when he had kissed her for the first time. With his cocky, challenging grin, Sonny had carried her through a multitude of firsts.

He always would, Cyndi resolved.

But how she wished things were still as simple as they'd been in junior high.

The song on the radio changed to a softer tune, and Cyndi turned to Sonny. "Do you think about the future much?"

"The future?"

"College, coming back here to Hazelhurst."

Sonny's face hardened. "I don't want to come back here."

"Not come back? But the bank—"

"Would probably get along without me."

"Your father would be disappointed."

"He'd get over it."

"But Sonny—"

"Listen, Cyndi," he said, "I don't want to talk about my dad, okay? I don't want to make plans or worry about college. That's all we've done for the past couple of months."

"We had to make decisions."

"And we did." Sonny wheeled the car down the long, tree-lined driveway to the country club where the prom was always held. "In three months, I'm going dutifully off to Ohio University, just the way you and my parents want me to."

Terror squeezed her chest. "You don't want to go?"

Tight-lipped, he guided the car to a stop in the parking lot. "Can we just drop it, Cyndi? Can we just go in there and have some fun with our friends? It seems like nothing's ever any fun anymore." He got out of the car and slammed the door.

Instead of waiting for him to help her out, Cyndi opened her own door and met him near the front of the car. Desperation clawed at her insides as she put her hands against his chest. "I'm sorry," she murmured, her fingers curling around the lapels of his tuxedo jacket. "Please, Sonny, I don't mean to be a drag. I want to have some fun, too. I want it to be the way it's always been. I'm sorry, I—"

"Oh, Cyndi." Her name was little more than a sigh as his arms went around her. His lips skimmed her forehead.

Tipping her head back, she gazed up at him. "I hate it when you're mad at me. And I don't want to fight tonight. Tonight, I want..." Though she tried hard, as she had done several times this evening, the decision she had made about tonight refused to move past her dry throat. It didn't seem right to just say it, baldly, without preamble or preparation. The right moment would come after the prom.

Sonny put a hand to her cheek. Lightly he touched her upswept hair. "The princess looks all grown-up tonight."

"She is," Cyndi whispered. Then she stepped away. "Come on, let's go inside and have some fun."

As they moved into the club's elegant ballroom, Sonny seemed to be his usual self, cutting up with the guys, complimenting even the plainest girls. But his laughter was forced, his comments were too loud, his smile too bright. In contrast, Cyndi grew quieter as they joined Jennifer and Ryder at one of the small circular tables arranged to one side of the ballroom.

Jennifer bubbled and effused, accepting compliments on her prom committee's decorations and the sound of the outlandishly dressed band. Ryder was his usual silent self, his mouth quirked in amusement as he watched the steady parade of classmates who stopped to pay court at their table.

It wasn't unlike dozens of other evenings they had all shared. They danced and carried on and gossiped. But everything was just slightly off kilter. Like last Saturday when Sonny had dragged them all to the lake, tension settled over them like a net.

What's wrong with us? Cyndi wondered when one of those odd, unnerving silences fell.

"There's Meredith," Jennifer chirped, looking as if their friend's appearance was of global importance. She jumped up, waving. "I'll go get her."

"God, what a nerd," Sonny muttered as Cyndi stood and waved to Meredith, too.

Thinking he referred to Jennifer, Cyndi looked at him in surprise. "Who's a nerd?"

"That Craig creep Meredith's with," Sonny retorted.

Cyndi had never thought of Craig Smythe as a creep or a nerd. Student council president and voted Most Likely to Succeed, Craig would attend Harvard on a scholarship this fall.

Sonny turned to Ryder and jerked his head in Craig's direction. "Get a load of his stupid white tux."

Ryder, whose gaze didn't stray from where Jennifer stood talking with Meredith and Craig, shuddered. "I guess Meredith's making do with second best, too, Sonny-boy."

Confused by Ryder's meaning, Cyndi missed what Sonny said next, but it made Ryder look at him. Eyes narrowed, voice lowering, he said, "Just give me a reason, Sonny-boy, any reason at all."

"Sonny!" Cyndi caught his arm as he stood. He tried to shake her off, but she clung to him, smiling at those at nearby tables who turned to look at them. "What's wrong with you? Everyone's watching."

Glancing around, he seemed to need a moment to realize where they were. "Sorry," he mumbled, but he drew away from Cyndi.

She took her seat again, anxiously watching Ryder, who was still glaring at Sonny.

Sonny sat, too, again smiling and nodding at couples who passed their table on the way to the dance floor. A pretty, dark-haired girl, part of the class's rougher crowd, smiled at him, straightening her shoulders so that her full breasts pushed against the bodice of her tight red formal. Sonny grinned back.

Cyndi stared at him in horror. Then she remembered the taunts he had thrown at her during some of their worst arguments. *"Other girls aren't so uptight, Cyndi. Other girls don't say no."*

Had this girl said yes? On those nights when Cyndi resisted Sonny, had he found solace with someone else?

She had never believed he would. In her tidy little world, there had never been room for the possibility of another girl. Sure, Sonny flirted with everyone. Even Meredith and Jennifer. But it didn't mean anything. He had dated other girls, just as Cyndi had been out with other boys. But she had always known it would be Sonny in the end. Automatically her hand went to the class ring she usually wore on a chain. In deference to her formal, it was on her hand tonight, heavy and solid, narrowed to fit her finger by layers of tape. That ring was proof of who she was, where she belonged. At Sonny's side.

Without Sonny, who would she be?

Her head began to pound in rhythm with the loud music, and she closed her eyes, opening them to catch what could have been sympathy in Ryder's eyes. That stiffened her spine. She wasn't giving Sonny up without a fight. She scooted her chair closer to his just as Jennifer, Meredith and Craig appeared. She tried to laugh and joke. She tried to create the fun Sonny had said he wanted.

But it didn't come.

And soon Cyndi's perception of the evening began to resemble a distorted scene in a fun-house mirror. She danced—with everyone, not just Sonny. She posed for photographs with the entire gang. She was left with impressions—Meredith's sad blue eyes, the screech of the band's guitars, the higher-than-normal pitch of Jennifer's giggles.

One by one people began to disappear. Jennifer and Ryder. Meredith and Craig. Then Sonny was gone, too, leaving her alone with the remnants of the crowd. Trying to swallow the sickeningly sweet punch someone had brought her, Cyndi sat ramrod straight. She smiled at no one and nothing in particular and stared at the banner swaying over the bandstand. One Moment in Time, it proclaimed, the theme of tonight's dance. The bright blue letters were as shiny as they'd been at the beginning of the evening, but the banner had slipped and hung crooked now. Fittingly crooked, Cyndi thought.

"Let's go."

The grip on her shoulder made her jump. She looked up into Sonny's handsome face. His smile was fleeting. "Aren't you ready to go?" he asked. Feeling numb, she followed.

Forever after, Cyndi could never remember the walk to Sonny's car. She remembered, however, the stop light where the road to Crystal Lake turned off the main highway. There, while they were stopped, she took hold of the steering wheel. "I want to go to the lake, Sonny. I want to talk."

"But the party—"

"I don't care about the party," Cyndi said, letting her voice rise. "I have something I want to talk about."

Several cars turned toward the lake, and as their headlights washed the interior of the car, Cyndi could clearly see Sonny's face. In his expression, she thought she saw fear. He sat staring at her while cars behind them began to sound their horns.

"Sonny? Sonny, are you okay?"

In answer, he turned right, toward Crystal Lake.

It wasn't long before he pulled the car to a stop beside his parents' darkened summer house. Around them, the trees rustled in the cool spring breeze. The moon was full, sparkling off the surface of the lake and the car's hood.

Cyndi felt Sonny turn toward her. She could sense him waiting, and suddenly the close confines of the car seemed too small. "Let's get out," she suggested.

Sonny came around to help her out, but he said nothing as they stood beside his car. He was nervous. Cyndi could tell because of the way he kept running his hands through his hair. He took off his tie and stuck it into his pocket. He looked everywhere but at her.

She thought about asking about the girl at the dance. But whatever had happened didn't matter now. What was important was how Cyndi handled the next few minutes. She didn't know what to say. So in the end, she kissed Sonny. Calling on all the ardor she had banked and ignored and fought for years, she kissed him hard.

But he held her away. "Cyndi, what is it?"

"Like you said, Sonny, I'm finally all grown-up." She took a deep breath, released it. "And I want you. Just the way you say you want me."

"But Cyndi—"

"I decided last Saturday, after that last big fight about this, I knew then that I really was just being silly. We're not kids anymore. We've been dating a long time, and..." Cyndi paused, knowing she was rambling on, wishing Sonny would say something, *anything*. "Please, Sonny, I—"

He cut off her entreaty with a kiss, a deep kiss, full of the sweet, coaxing pressure she had come to know. Rather clumsily, he tumbled her hair to her shoulders. He turned her against the car, his hands slipping over her. So tenderly. So gently. Cyndi responded, waiting for the forbidden pleasure to flood every secret, hidden part of her, as it had so many times. Yet all she could think of was the girl in the red dress at the dance.

"Sonny," she whispered, drawing his face to hers. "There's not anyone else, is there, Sonny?"

He stepped back. "What do you mean?"

"Someone else," Cyndi repeated. "There isn't anyone, is there?"

Sonny swore. "Ryder said something, didn't he?"

Like ice, fear wrapped around Cyndi's heart. "What would Ryder know to say?"

"Nothing," Sonny retorted quickly. Too quickly. "He doesn't know anything. But I know how he's always shooting his mouth off."

"But he didn't say anything, Sonny. I just..." Cyndi paused, shaking her head.

"Don't worry," Sonny murmured, taking her hand and pulling her close again. "Don't think about anything. Tonight is all that matters." Again his mouth covered hers.

Cyndi tried to concentrate on Sonny's kiss. She tried to ignore the tiny voice inside her that told her this wasn't right. She fought the voice for a long time. For endless minutes she clung instead to Sonny's husky whispers, which told her what *he* wanted, what she *should* want.

She did her best, but when it felt as if the two voices were ripping her in two, she pulled away. Sonny, laughing, only held her tighter, his touch growing more intimate. Finally she pushed him. Hard.

"Hey," he said, catching both her hands. "What's wrong? I thought you said..."

"I know, but—"

"You can't do that," Sonny muttered. "You can't just keep changing course on a guy."

"But I'm not sure. I'm not..."

For a moment, he was still. Then he brought her close. And there was nothing gentle about his kiss. There was nothing familiar about the way he touched her or the way he pushed her against the car.

Genuinely frightened, Cyndi struggled against him. "Sonny, you're hurting me. Let me go—"

He flung her away from him then, slinging her so hard she had to grab the edge of the front grillwork to keep from falling to the ground. Her shoe caught in her hem, ripping it, while her heart broke at the names Sonny called her.

"Sonny," she whispered. "Please. Stop..."

His voice rose. "Tonight of all nights, Cyndi, why'd you have to play games?"

"Maybe you think sex is a game, Sonny. I don't. That's not what I was brought up to think."

"Yeah, that's right," he said coldly. "Your game isn't sex. It's called tease. That's all you ever do. All you can do."

Unshed tears scalded Cyndi's eyes. She blinked them away. "I just can't—"

"Can't. Don't. Shouldn't. That's all you ever say."

"But it's the way I feel," Cyndi protested. "And if you loved me, you'd understand. You'd wait until I'm ready. I love you, Sonny—"

"Love?" He spat the word at her. "You're not capable of love. You're just as cold and frigid as your mother."

"Sonny!"

"Why do you think I went looking for other girls, Cyndi? You turned me away—"

She began backing away. "Please, don't—"

"Nobody knows it to look at you. You're so beautiful. All the guys are hot for you, but they don't know you like I do—"

"Sonny, stop it!"

"You're the reason I'm in this mess right now—"

"Sonny, please shut up!" Cyndi's voice echoed through the trees, at last silencing him. It was probably the first time she had ever yelled at him. She wanted to do it again. She wanted to hit him, to hurt him in some small measure as he was hurting her.

"This is your fault," he whispered finally, brokenly, forcing her to look at him. "If you hadn't pushed me, Cyndi..."

"Take me home," she commanded, marching toward the car.

"Cyndi—"

In answer, she got in the car, slamming the door.

It was over.

Over.

That knowledge beat in her head during the silent ride back to Hazelhurst. Sonny broke every traffic law in the book, but Cyndi didn't care. All she could hear were those ugly words he had tossed at her.

You're not capable of love. You're cold. Frigid. Just like your mother.

A tiny questioning part of her began to wonder if he was right.

Feeling dazed, it was a moment before she realized they had pulled up in front of the school gymnasium.

"I'm going to the party," Sonny muttered. "Everyone's expecting us."

"I don't care. I want to go home."

"And face your mother?" His laugh was unpleasant. "Sure, Cyndi. You go right on home." Thinking of her mother's displeasure, Cyndi said nothing. Sonny leaned across her and flipped the sunshade down to reveal a lighted mirror. "Here, you can fix your face."

With trembling hands, she did what she could with her hair and makeup. Then, clutching the overnight bag that held a change of clothes, she followed Sonny to the gym's door.

The familiar, rather shabby, gymnasium had been transformed into a tropical paradise by parents of the seniors. Palm trees and hula girls were scattered about. A disk jockey was playing hits from the past four years on a sound system in the center. Everywhere kids—Cyndi's friends—having changed into casual clothes, were dancing and laughing, carrying on as if everything was just as it had always been.

But it wasn't.

At the door, Sonny turned to her. There was pain in his expression. Pain and loss and something else. Desperation, maybe, although she didn't know what he had to be desperate about. She wanted to say something to him. But she wasn't sure what that would be. So they stood there, together but not touching, in the doorway, until finally, Sonny headed off through the crowd. Cyndi watched until his blond hair disappeared in the swirl of lights and bright, tropical clothes.

And she knew nothing would ever be right again.

Ignoring the voices that called her name, she turned her back on the gym and went to the phone in the hall. She called home, told her father she was ill and asked to be picked up. Sonny would bring her, she lied brightly, but his car was acting up and besides, he was having such a good time. She didn't want to ruin his fun.

From the sound system, a song from freshman year blared. "Don't look back," the singer implored.

Cyndi didn't.

In Sonny's car, she left his class ring.

And she didn't cry that night.

The tears—and the guilt—came the next morning. When she found out he was dead.

Chapter Five

So now Cyndi had her own interview horror story.

Hands shoved deep into his pockets, Nick stood beside Lin and watched Cyndi deal with her temperamental guest. The actress, in her patented flamboyant manner, had taken control of the interview from the first question. Cyndi hadn't seized the reins again, although she had tried. Nick gave her full credit for trying.

"We'll edit," Lin muttered almost under her breath as Cyndi began the wrap-up. "We'll make this look as smooth as cream."

Nick merely nodded as Lin moved away, scribbling notes on a clipboard. He knew a session in the editing booth could even out the rough edges on this segment, but he was sorry it was necessary. But most of all, he wished he hadn't come to today's taping.

Even though he was the executive in charge of this production, he wasn't needed on the set every day. He had enough confidence in Lin and Joe and the rest of the crew to know a real disaster would never make it on the air. So he should have stayed away. He didn't need to see the disappointment now marring Cyndi's features. It made him want to do something terribly inappropriate—like put his arms around her and kiss the unhappiness from her soft, pretty mouth.

Kissing Cyndi. Damn, but that was an appealing notion. It had been his impulse weeks ago, at her house. It had intensified last night before she had bolted like a frightened child from his car. It was even more of a temptation now. And Nick didn't want to be tempted by Cyndi. He had spent half the day trying to erase the memory of her scent, trying to forget the hurt in her blue eyes when she talked of her mother's unfulfilled expectations. That same hurt shadowed her gaze now as she bade a polite goodbye to her guest and fled the studio. Nick told himself to just let her alone.

He repeated that all the way to her closed dressing room door.

Not bothering to knock, he found Cyndi standing in front of the mirror where last night she had so steadfastly prepared for today's task.

Their gazes met in the mirror before she looked away. "Just don't say it. You don't have to."

He clicked the door shut behind him. "What do you think I'm about to say?"

"Cut the bull, okay? We both know I screwed up." With jerky movements, she tugged the pins out of her upswept hairdo. Her hair—that wonderful, silky mass of gold—fell about her shoulders. Jealously Nick watched her fingers brush through the tangled curls. His hands clenched into fists at his sides.

"I let her ramble," Cyndi continued. "I wasn't crisp or precise enough with my questions. She took over. And I let her." Impatiently she jerked off the colorful scarf that had been draped so artfully across her blue jacket. "I can't believe I let her get the upper hand. How stupid can I be?" The jacket followed the scarf to a chair, where they both slid unheeded to the floor.

"I've seen worse," Nick said mildly, stooping to pick up the discarded clothes.

"Do me a favor," Cyndi said. "Don't humor me. Just tell me how terrible I was and then leave me alone."

"I don't think I have to tell you anything. Sounds like you know what you did wrong."

"Wrong? It was worse than wrong. It was pitiful."

Nick dropped the jacket and scarf over the chair's back again. "Pitiful? I don't know if I'd go that far."

"But it was," Cyndi insisted, her face flushed with anger. "I was just as bad as you've been saying I'd be. You were right. Oh, God . . ." She stepped out of her shoes and kicked them out of the way. "I was so darn bad." She undid the buckle on her belt. "I've never—"

"Cyndi," Nick cut in, "I hate to interrupt, but are you going to keep undressing?" Her startled gaze snapped up to his. "I mean, I don't mind, not at all, but I just want to know."

Her flush deepened.

"Really, it's okay." Grinning, he turned the chair around. "Just hold it there for a minute and let me get a good seat." He sat down, his arms resting on the chair's back. "Now, go on. What were you saying?"

Totally discomfited, Cyndi just stood, gaping at him. *What in the world was she doing? Lord, she really was losing it.*

"Well," Nick urged, "go on."

Cyndi began rebuckling her belt just as Lin walked in.

Lin's mouth formed an O as she gazed from Nick to Cyndi and back again. He laughed. Cyndi choked.

Pausing with her hand on the doorknob, Lin said, "I think I'm going to go back in the hall, knock and come in again."

"Don't be silly." Cyndi hastily rooted for the shoes she had kicked away. "Nick and I were just…just…"

"Going over some interview pointers," he supplied.

"Oh." Still looking uncertain, Lin stepped inside. "I just wanted to see if you were okay, Cyndi. It was rough out there today."

Cyndi breathed a disgruntled sigh. "I'm sorry. I let everyone down."

Lin dismissed the apology with a flip of her hand. "The woman is a viper."

"I knew that. I should have been prepared."

"Well, what's done is done," Lin said. "I won't lie to you and say it's the best interview ever. But with a few cuts here and there, it'll play just fine."

"It won't happen again."

Nick shook his head. "Yes, it will. There'll be other vipers. You'll make more mistakes."

Cyndi straightened her shoulders. "I know that's what you expect from me, Nick."

"It's what I'd expect from anyone. No one person can be a hundred percent perfect all the time." He frowned, searching her defiant features. "I expect you to be damn good, yes. If there are too many days like today we're in trouble. But you can't be perfect all the time. Much as I expect from everyone who works for me, I don't expect the impossible. And if that's what you expect from yourself, you're going to be more and more disappointed."

"Exactly," Lin agreed. "So you weren't at your best today." She shrugged. "You'll get 'em next time."

When Cyndi started to protest again, Nick said softly, "You fought a good fight, Cyndi. Now put it to rest."

She was silent, oddly pleased that he shared his family's special compliment with her.

Lin cleared her throat. "I'm needed elsewhere, so I'm going to leave now." The smile she gave Cyndi was just slightly quizzical. Promising to call over the weekend, she left.

Alone again with Nick, Cyndi said, "Thanks for being so understanding about the interview. You could be acting smug at this point."

Picking up her scarf, he shrugged. "What would that accomplish? Besides, you were doing a good job beating yourself up without my help." He grinned and his voice deepened. "Now, what were we doing before Lin interrupted?"

Watching the fragile silk material being threaded through his strong, distinctly male hands made Cyndi swallow. She attempted a feeble explanation about her discarded clothes. "After we tape our other show, Lin always comes back here and we talk, and . . ."

"I hate to tell you this, Queenie." Nick's smile robbed the nickname of its sarcasm. "But I'm not much like Lin." He stood, dropping the scarf again and shoving the chair in place under her makeup table. Cyndi let her gaze travel up the gray slacks and blue shirt that hinted at the muscles beneath. Nick might dress carelessly, but he had a good body. A supremely masculine body.

He turned, caught her assessing regard and, to Cyndi's consternation, winked. The gesture, coming from this man, was incongruous.

Flushed and feeling like a genuine fool, Cyndi started for her desk, rambling an excuse, "I'm just all stressed out. Not thinking clearly. I'm a mess if I don't get in my workout every day, and today's been too hectic. What I need to do is get out, go for a run, get some exercise—"

"Wear this."

She turned just as a black leotard and tights landed on her desk. Nick had taken them from a peg on the wall. Puzzled, she looked up at him.

"You're right," he said. "You're tense and upset. It's been a stressful week, a stressful month. You need to work off some of your frustrations. I'll show you how."

"You'll show me?"

"Don't think I can?"

She wasn't sure what to make of the challenging gleam in his dark eyes. "Nick..."

"I'll meet you downstairs in ten minutes," he said, heading for the door. "After I check in with my office."

"But I still have things to do here."

He turned at the door. "It's Friday afternoon, and you're taking off. My orders."

His orders. He had some nerve. "I didn't know the boss had a right to dictate my free time."

"Consider this research—a new workout idea."

It would have been sensible of her to refuse. But Cyndi wasn't feeling sensible. The thought of a second evening with Nick was infinitely more appealing than an evening with her cat and a cable TV movie.

"Okay," she agreed. "But this is getting to be a habit. Last night. Tonight."

His smile flashed as he opened the door. "Mama taught me to cultivate good habits."

And his father had taught him to box.

That much was evident as Cyndi stood in a gym an hour later, watching Nick work out his own frustrations on a punching bag. Sweat glistened on the tanned arms and shoulders revealed by his sleeveless black T-shirt. Beneath abbreviated gray shorts, his legs were as muscular as she had suspected. If this was what Nick did to stay in shape, it certainly worked, though the gym was a far cry from the exclusive sports clubs an executive might be expected to attend. In fact, Cyndi hadn't known gyms like this existed outside the late show and a few Sylvester Stallone movies.

Shouts of encouragement and the slap of leather against leather filled the cavernous but crowded room. When she and Nick had walked in the door, the greetings had made it obvious he was a regular. Just as it was obvious women weren't regulars. Cyndi had earned more than her share of stares, even though she hadn't removed the long, hip-tied T-shirt she had worn over her tights and leotard. No one had directed any disrespectful comments toward her, although the majority of the language was as colorful as the decor was bland. Gray walls and gray floor surrounded several rings and workout areas. The smell of perspiration mixed with liniment. The entire masculine domain was presided over by the stocky, white-haired owner who was holding Nick's punching bag. A man with the improbable name of Sweet Pea Potter.

Sweet Pea's smile was a slash of white in his ebony face. "Nick could've turned pro," he called to Cyndi. "He's got a better right hook than his daddy ever had."

Cyndi smiled and nodded, not knowing what else to say. Nick gave the bag a final punch and dashed the perspiration from his face with his forearm. "Come on, Sweet Pea," he got out between gasps. "You know Pop was better than me."

The man's smile grew broader. "But you're meaner, Nick."

"I'll buy that," Cyndi put in, grinning at Nick.

Sweet Pea chuckled. "That was his daddy's downfall. He wasn't mean enough."

"Do you have to be mean to make it big, Sweet Pea?"

He nodded. "A killer instinct, that's what it takes. But Nick's daddy, shoot, all he had on his mind was gettin' through and gettin' home to his family. Me and the boys, we called him Lonely Tony Calderaro. Man was handsome, a sight better lookin' than this son of his. And the women." He whistled. "He could've had any of 'em. But he was always thinkin' 'bout his Rosa. So it was for the best when Tony settled down with his little gym."

"Was your father's place like this?" Cyndi asked Nick.

He shook his head, glancing around. "Smaller. After Sweet Pea retired from the ring, he worked there with Pop, training some pretty good young fighters."

The older man threw up his hands. "They were losers, Nick, losers, not a contender in the bunch. They had no heart. I got tired of them and those cold Boston winters. When you're from Memphis, that cold almost freezes your soul."

"So you struck out for California, didn't you, old man?"

"Old man?" Sweet Pea drew himself up to his full height. "Who you callin' old, son? You shouldn't be forgettin' I used to tan your hide when you came down to the gym, carryin' on, raisin' a ruckus. I bet I could tan it now."

"I'm sure you could," Nick agreed, grinning as he stripped off his gloves. "Pop never could."

"That's your problem. Nobody ever gave you a lick exceptin' me and your mama." Sweet Pea shook his head, turning to Cyndi. "This scamp here had four big sisters wrapped around his finger. Those silly girls took the blame for half the mischief he caused. His daddy thought he could do no wrong. Only his mama and me knew what to do with him.''

Cyndi cut her gaze toward Nick. "So you were spoiled rotten, were you?"

"So Sweet Pea thinks," Nick retorted. The two men smiled at each other with obvious affection, a gesture that warmed Cyndi. She glanced at Nick, thinking he was a surprising man, not at all the cold perfectionist he had seemed at first.

"Come on," he said to her now. "It's your turn with the bag."

"I don't think..."

"You don't have to think. Just punch." He gave her a gentle push toward the bag. "Sweet Pea, let's get some gloves on her."

The older man shook his head. "Man alive, it's somethin' when pretty ladies start comin' to the gym to work out. Before you know it I'll have aye-robic classes for the boys."

Nick chuckled. "Could be a potential job opportunity, Cyndi. Keep it in mind if the show doesn't work out."

"Oh, you..." She glared at him as Sweet Pea helped her put on the gloves.

"Ready to punch something now?" Nick teased, swinging the bag in her direction.

A few moments and a couple of instructions later, Cyndi laid her first tentative punch into the bag.

The impact made her arm sting, but Nick wasn't satisfied. "Come on," he implored, "you can do better than that. Punch it. Put something behind it."

She walloped it harder.

"Better. But you can do it harder. Pretend the bag is your troubles."

She gave the bag a fair imitation of the one-two punch Nick had shown her. "That was today's interview."

"Good. Now really lay into that viper."

Visualizing the actress's pretty face etched into the bag, Cyndi socked it again, pleased with the feeling of power it brought.

"All your problems," Nick prompted. "You make the bag into all your problems. Then you hit 'em. Hard."

All her problems. What came to mind first were the memories that followed her everywhere she went these days. Gritting her teeth, she concentrated, turning the bag into her past. She tore into the solid weight, chipping away at her guilt over Sonny's death. She smashed all the mistakes that had dogged her heels ever since. Her hasty, ill-fated marriage. Her divorce. Her mother's disapproval. The career she had fallen into. She punched and punched, not expecting it to make any difference. But it did. There was something exhilarating about pummeling those mistakes with her fists. Something primitive. Violent. Quite apart from her normal self.

With Nick calling out encouragement, she punched the bag until her blood was pumping, till her arms ached and her shoulders throbbed. And when she stopped, Nick grabbed her by the waist and twirled her around.

"See!" he whooped. "It felt good, didn't it? Didn't you feel it, Cyndi?"

Instead of pausing for an answer, he kissed her.

Cyndi wasn't sure what had made her dizzy—the punching, the twirling or the kiss. But as her arms traveled around Nick's neck, she decided it was the latter. Definitely the latter. She should have known how dizzying Nick Calderaro's kiss would be. Closing her eyes, she focused on the sweet pressure of his lips against her own. Dear heaven, she felt like a runner on her last lap, with the fine sting of victory pumping adrenaline through her muscles.

It was the silence that made Nick draw away. The gym's normal din had faded sometime after his mouth had touched Cyndi's. Already knowing what he'd find, he looked up. They were the object of every stare in the place, and he had to wonder what had happened to his self-restraint.

Sweet Pea's voice was low, "Lawsy-day, Nick. See what happens when I break my rules and let a woman in my gym?" Whistling, he strolled away, and, as if on cue, everyone's attention returned to their own business.

Her face pressed close to Nick's shoulder, Cyndi whispered, "Please tell me everyone isn't staring."

"They aren't. Not now, anyway."

She stepped away, her face flaming red, but Nick caught her hand. He drew her back into the circle of his arms. "I'm sorry," he murmured. "I didn't mean to make such a public display. Cyndi, look at me." With hand under her chin, he turned her face up to his. "I didn't intend that to happen."

"Neither did I."

"But aren't you glad?" he asked, grinning. "Aren't you glad to have it out of the way?" She looked puzzled. "The first time's the hardest."

"The first?"

"Of many more." Her blue eyes widened. Nick brushed her cheek with the gentlest of kisses. One hand went to her hair, tangling in the soft curls he had longed to touch for so long. Desire shot through him. Hot, undeniable desire. Pulling away without kissing her again took a monumental effort. "Let's go somewhere," he whispered.

"Where?"

"Someplace where fifty people aren't watching us."

They went to her place. His apartment was closer, but as he followed her car through the warm California evening Nick's urgency cooled. He knew he couldn't be impatient with Cyndi. He had to take care, great care. If he started making demands, she would back away.

At her house, Cyndi directed Nick to the guest room bath for a shower. Since she had taken the time to shower at the studio, she concentrated on starting dinner. She kept her hands busy—marinating chicken breasts in teriyaki sauce, turning on the gas grill, chopping vegetables for a salad.

Her mind worked as well, conjuring visions of Nick's hard, male body being pelted by a warm spray of water. She pictured his sinewy arms. The tanned column of his throat. She could see herself kissing the hollow right at the base... The image grew so detailed her hands began to tremble. The paring knife she held clattered to the tiled counter. Cyndi closed her eyes and leaned forward, drawing a deep breath. What was she doing? Fantasies about Nick would lead nowhere. Nowhere.

And just where did she want them to lead?

The question opened her eyes. She turned at the sound of the kitchen door swishing open and closed. Pausing beside the table, Nick smiled at her as he tucked in his shirt. His dark hair was wet, curling around his forehead, an oddly boyish counterpoint to the normally harsh planes of his face. He wore the same gray dress slacks and blue shirt as before, but the shirt's top buttons were undone, the sleeves rolled up. He looked relaxed—and amused.

With the illogical feeling that he knew exactly what she had been imagining about him, Cyndi demanded, "What's so funny?"

"Your cat." Nick pointed to the floor, where Lolita was rubbing herself against his leg. "It seems she's had a reversal of opinion since the last time I was here."

"She's fickle as well as precocious."

"Whatever the case, she certainly had a fine time watching me shower."

Again a vivid, entirely erotic image sprang to Cyndi's mind. Wheeling around, she grabbed the knife and attacked some mushrooms with a vengeance. "For some reason Lolita likes bathtubs. She's always poking her nose around my shower curtain or sitting on the edge of my hot tub. Most cats hate water, but not her."

"And here I thought you had just told her to like me." Nick stepped closer, but Cyndi didn't turn around or even look up from her task. His voice dropped. "I mean, you have changed your opinion about me, haven't you?"

The lightness Cyndi forced into her tone was a triumph of will over emotion. "You mean do I like you, Mr. Calderaro? Of course. You're the boss." A touch on her shoulder stilled the motion of her knife. Nick stepped close enough for her to feel the warmth from his body along her back.

"Is that why I'm here?" he whispered, an unexpected sharpness in his voice. "Because I'm the boss? I was kidding about that earlier, Cyndi. This...us...it has nothing to do with the show. If you really hadn't wanted to come tonight—"

"I know." She turned her head to the side. Nick was close. So very disturbingly close. That made it hard for her to organize her chaotic thoughts. "I was kidding, too."

His breath fanned her cheek. His hands settled on her arms. The touch jolted Cyndi, made her catch her breath.

Nick pressed his cheek to her hair. "I don't usually do this."

"This?"

"Get involved with people I work with."

Involved. Was that what this was? An involvement? The word reminded Cyndi of her lack of success when it came to entanglements. Strange how one kiss had made her forget that. Dropping her knife again, she turned in Nick's arms, facing him. "Please, let's not..."

He cut her off. "I just wanted to make things clear. I found out the hard way that it's best to keep your work and your personal life separate. I don't want any work conflicts between us."

There was something in his eyes, in the bitter set of his mouth that told her he had been hurt. Badly. She was amazed by the sympathy that welled inside her. "I'm sorry," she said.

And Nick smiled, the movement chasing all hint of bitterness from his face. "And Cyndi being sorry could almost make everything okay." He lifted a hand to her face, his thumb trailing across her mouth. "How do you do it? You smile and the whole world seems to stop."

"I don't do that."

His frown was puzzled, as if he didn't know quite what to make of her. "Yes, that's exactly what you do."

Her next words were caught beneath the pressure of his mouth. The kiss was gentle at first, almost teasing. That quickly changed. With lips and tongue, Nick coaxed. Cyndi acquiesced. Her hands slipped up his arms, across his shoulders, coming to rest in the soft, damp hair that curled against his neck. She breathed in the soap-and-water scent of his skin. And with a groan, she let Nick take her deeper into passion. His kiss absorbed her, heated her, overwhelmed her senses.

She wasn't sure she had ever been kissed like this. With such abandon, with such relentless fire. She was certain the response of her body had never been so keen, so fast. A nameless ache uncurled inside her, spiraling in all directions. Through the thin knit of her leotard she acknowledged the undeniable pressure of Nick's growing need. And sanity began to return. She had to stop. She wasn't ready for this. Harsh experience had taught her about foolish impulses and their inevitable disappointments.

"Nick," she whispered, turning from his kiss. "Please..."

He rested his forehead against her hair for a moment. But he did pull away. Cyndi expected annoyance or anger. She expected anything but his smile.

He said, "On the drive over, I told myself this wasn't going to happen. But then you had to stand here, looking so...so kissable."

Nick brushed a strand of hair from her cheek and watched her lashes sweep down, screening her reaction. Her hands fluttered nervously as she turned back to the counter. With any other woman he would think the discomfiture an artifice. But not with Cyndi. Her uncertainty was one quality that made her so very fascinating. Half child, half woman, she seemed unsure of herself, wary of the sexual current running between them.

For a moment she stood, staring out the window. Then she looked at him, frowning. "I don't know quite what to make of this...of us."

"Then don't make anything of it. Just let it happen."

She shook her head. "I don't do things that way."

"Maybe you should."

"And maybe I'm just like you. Maybe I don't want to get involved with a colleague, either."

Hip braced against the counter, he crossed his arms. "You're already involved."

She looked up, her blue eyes startled. "A couple of kisses don't make an involvement."

"Is that all we have here—a couple of kisses?"

"What do you think?"

"I'm not sure," he admitted. "But I know I want to figure it out. I want to figure you out."

"But there's nothing to figure...."

"Nothing to figure? Lady, you're a mystery. The deepest, most intriguing mystery I've run into since I first discovered sex."

"Is sex all there is to it? Is that what you want from me?"

"I don't think it would be enough." His words surprised even Nick. For most of his adult life, he had known exactly what he wanted from women—either sex or companionship. Rarely both. When he had wanted everything, the woman hadn't had it to give. The thought of wanting that again was almost frightening.

Cyndi was regarding him warily. Too warily. He forced himself to relax. "Do we have to work all of this out right now?" Grinning, he added, "I mean, you've got the food almost ready. If we're going to argue or something, I'd rather wait until after dinner." He picked up the pan of marinating chicken. "What do I do with these?"

Cyndi decided not to push. Nick was right. They didn't need all the answers right now. She wasn't even certain what her questions were. Once again, she had stumbled into something she didn't quite understand.

What did she want from this man? Nick Calderaro was more of a mystery than she would ever be. One moment he was so tough, so demanding. The next he could tease a person into forgetting their troubles. He did just that as they finished the dinner preparations. Expertly, without apparent effort, he made her talk about herself, leading the conversation from food to childhood memories.

They ate on the deck outside the dining area. The day had been a rare beauty, virtually smog-free. The breeze was cool enough to be pleasant, slight enough to allow candles on the table. It was easy to relax. Prompted by Nick, Cyndi talked about growing up in Hazelhurst.

"It was so very Midwest," she said finally, staring pensively at the wine she swirled in her glass. "Not much like your childhood in Boston, I'm sure."

"I doubt they were so very different." He got up and stood beside the deck railing, apparently studying the lights from the other houses that spread down the hillside of Cyndi's neighborhood. The glow from the iron lanterns placed at intervals around the deck cast his face in half shadow as he turned around. "One thing's for sure, in neither Massachusetts or Ohio would we be dining alfresco in February."

Cyndi nodded. "I talked to my father before I came to the studio this morning. It was snowing."

Hazelhurst in the snow. She had only to close her eyes to see the white roof of the two-story home where she had grown up. The holly bushes around the porch would be heavy with snow. And inside, it would be quiet and warm, with the furnace humming and flames crackling in the fireplace in her father's study. He would get up early tomorrow to clear the driveway and sidewalk. She worried about him working so hard out in the cold. He laughed at her concern, saying he was fit and healthy. He wasn't an old man, after all. But her mother hadn't been old either, and she was gone.

Nick's quiet voice intruded on her thoughts. "Do you miss home, Cyndi?"

Shaking off her melancholy thoughts, she replied, "This is my home. I haven't lived in Hazelhurst since the summer I was eighteen."

"Is that when you came to California?"

"No, I went to college." She set her glass on the table, considering whether to tell the rest of the story. Why not? Failed marriages weren't rarities. Not everyone shared her deep sense of shame. Taking a deep breath, she plunged ahead, "After my freshman year I got married."

There was a pause from Nick. "You were very young."

"We both were. But he was a football hero, a first-round draft pick with a big bonus, and he was moving to L.A. Marrying him seemed the best way to keep from losing him."

"Desperation isn't the best basis for a marriage."

The empathy in his voice made her glance up. Desperation, yes, that's what she had that entire year after Sonny's death. Desperate for someone to take his place, she had given her virginity to a handsome college football star and then married him in a burst of guilt and haste. Desperation had kept her going when nothing—not the young man, the sex or the marriage—had turned out as she'd expected. Nick sounded as if he knew the lengths to which desperation could push a person. "You don't have a hasty marriage in your past, too, do you?" she asked, getting up and joining him beside the deck railing.

"No, I never took the plunge, although I was tempted a time or two."

Cyndi sighed. "I learned quickly that marriage isn't something you rush into."

"What happened?"

Only later did she wonder why she opened up to Nick without hesitation. She never talked about her marriage, not even to Lin. But she told Nick about her June wedding and move to L.A. Her young husband, who was now a standout pro player, hadn't reacted well to the bonds of matrimony. He was away a lot, under pressure to live up to the money the team had invested in him. Cyndi, being young and immature, resented his absences. They argued and drifted apart.

"After two years, the marriage was over," she explained to Nick. She didn't tell him about her husband's blatant infidelities. Or the hurtful reasons he had given as an excuse for his behavior. "I got the house," she said brightly. "Keith got his freedom."

Nick said nothing. He just took her hand in his own.

Cyndi took a deep breath and looked up at the clear, star-dusted sky. "Sometimes I even forget I was married. It was so fleeting. Keith was chasing his dreams, and I was . . ."

"You were what?" Nick prompted.

She deliberated a moment, then whispered, "I was running away from my dreams."

Nick didn't press for details. Though she could almost see his mind turning her statement over and over, he merely held her hand and let the night noises blanket them. Cars hummed in the distance. Next door, a woman called for a child to come inside. It was pleasant. Comfortable. Cyndi thought she could sit here by Nick's side for a long time.

He broke the spell. "I should be going."

Without thinking Cyndi let her fingers curl against his, holding on. "It's not too late. Must you?"

"We have to get an early start tomorrow."

"We?"

"I thought we'd sail over to Catalina. Spend the rest of the weekend. How about it?"

The rest of the weekend. Day and night. Nick's nearness, so undemanding a moment ago, now seemed threatening. Especially when she remembered the kiss they had shared only a short while earlier.

"I know what you're thinking," he said. "And this isn't a plot to get you in my bed."

"That's not—"

"Yes, that is what you're thinking." Quickly, before she could protest, his hand brushed up her side, grazing her hip, following the curve of her breast and coming to rest against her cheek. Even in the shadows, she could see the look in his eyes was as steady as his touch. "I want you in my bed when you're ready to be there, Cyndi. You already know I don't like to play games."

"And you're very blunt."

"Honest," he corrected, grinning. "Come on, now. Go to Catalina with me this weekend. I have no hidden agendas. I just want to be with you."

How long had it been since a man had offered her such an uncomplicated invitation? Cyndi couldn't remember. She ignored the voice inside that said Nick Calderaro was anything but uncomplicated. Neither were the feelings he aroused in her. If she was sensible, she would stay home. But she wanted to go. She wanted to take a chance.

So she smiled at Nick and asked, "What time do we leave?"

Chapter Six

Nestled off the California coast in the blue-green waters of the Pacific, Santa Catalina Island had long been a magnet for tourists and locals longing to escape the Los Angeles urban sprawl. Midmorning Saturday, as Cyndi followed Nick aboard a boat at San Pedro, she felt she was escaping more than traffic jams and pollution. She was starting fresh. With no past. No expectations for the future. Today, there was only the perfect sky, the wind in her face and Nick's smile to warm her.

She slid into the seat he indicated and watched while he stowed their carryon bags underneath. In well-worn jeans, navy knit shirt and denim jacket, he looked comfortable today, much more at ease than usual. Thinking of his perpetually rumpled shirts and loosened ties made Cyndi smile.

He returned the favor. "Glad you came?"

"Very. I can't even remember the last time I got away like this."

"Then let's concentrate on having fun." As if to underscore his remark, the boat's motor revved and an excited buzz ran through the dozen or so people on board. Grinning, Nick sat back, his arm very naturally curving around her shoulders.

Cyndi didn't allow herself to question the rightness of that gesture. In regard to this weekend, she had made a promise to herself—well, to Devlin, too.

Her brother had come in from the hospital late last night, long after Nick had gone. Cyndi was still up, however, trying on half the clothes in her closet, already second-guessing her decision to go away for the weekend with Nick. She had fluttered around the kitchen and watched her brother finish up the left-over chicken and two bowls of chocolate frozen yogurt before she had asked his opinion.

And Devlin had laughed at her. "Good Lord, the man has asked you on a trip. It's not like he proposed or anything."

Cyndi sat down at the table and nervously pleated a paper napkin with her fingers. "But I'm spending the whole weekend with him, Dev. On a date you can just come home."

"You're not going to the ends of the earth. You can come home from Catalina, too. Unless, of course…" Devlin leaned forward, his gaze teasing. "Unless Nick ties you up and tortures you for the entire weekend."

"Please be serious."

DON'T LOOK BACK 123

"I am being serious. You never know what devious plans Nick might have in mind for the weekend." His grin grew broader as he ducked to avoid the napkin she threw at him. "Just make sure you take some condoms."

"Devlin!"

"Well, you're the one who said you barely knew him."

"Which is exactly why I'm not going to sleep with him."

"You could, you know."

"Oh, just be quiet." She got up, shoving her chair under the table and clattering dirty dishes together. "There's no use talking to you. You can't be serious for a minute."

"What's the big deal? If you and Nick are attracted to each other and if you're careful, what does it matter—"

She turned around and demanded, "Why is it you have so few problems talking about this?"

"You mean sex?"

"Right. We grew up in the same house, and I don't know how you turned out to be so freewheeling. I mean, if Mother could hear you . . ."

Devlin took the dishes from her and crossed to the sink. "Oh, she wouldn't be surprised. I was always the difficult one. You were perfect."

"Why do you say that? I'm the one who ran off to California and disgraced her by getting a d-i-v-o-r-c-e."

Devlin chuckled. "Yes, we must spell the shameful words, mustn't we? Or use euphemisms. Like 'expecting' for 'pregnant.' Poor Mother. Reality confused her so.''

"Confused her?"

"Sure." Devlin began rinsing dishes. "It was because of her own parents, I think." He shivered. "Remember when we'd go down and visit Grandmother? It was like being shut off from the rest of the world."

Cyndi nodded, thinking of the quiet, antique-filled house in Savannah, Georgia, where she and Devlin and their mother had spent several summers. There, the distant past had felt as close as yesterday. Tradition was sacred. Male and female roles were distinct, too. Little girls played quietly. Boys were allowed to run and jump and shout. Women gave tea parties and did volunteer work while men were doctors, lawyers and politicians. It was a careful world.

"Mother belonged there," Cyndi murmured.

"You'd think so," Devlin agreed. "But at some point she must have felt like rebelling. How else did she end up married to her cousin's Yankee roommate?" He grinned. "Of course, there's not too much of a mystery there, either. The Yankee was going home to a successful medical practice begun by his father. Mother moved into her own big house, even if it was in Ohio. She was a big deal in Hazelhurst. She wore the right clothes and drove the right car. She produced two healthy children. Dad adored her, let her do anything she wanted."

Devlin shook his head as he opened the dishwasher. "Mother never faced any really big problems. Life—the real, gritty facts of life brushed right past her." He paused, sadness touching his face. "Until the end, of course."

They fell silent. Their mother's sudden death two years before, after a bout with pneumonia, had left some unresolved issues between her and her children. For Cyndi more than Devlin, of course. She was the one who always sought their mother's approval.

"I wish I hadn't disappointed her," Cyndi said quietly.

"Is that still so important?"

"Yes...I mean, no." Cyndi sighed. "I guess I don't know, Dev."

He flipped the switch on the dishwasher and shrugged. "You gotta live for yourself, you know. So what if you didn't grow up and marry Sonny Keighton and live in the nicest house in Hazelhurst's North End."

Cyndi glanced at him in surprise. "How did you know that's what I wanted to do?"

"How could anyone have lived in our house and not known? It was 'Sonny this' and 'Sonny that' for years. Mother loved it, of course. He fit right into her world." He paused, as if considering his next words. "I always kind of thought Mother liked Sonny more than you did."

Cyndi was silent, thinking of how much Sonny had come to dislike her mother. To her dying day, she thought she would remember those hateful, ugly words he had said about her and her mother. *Cold. Not capable of love.*

Devlin's quiet voice snapped her out of the past. "Nick's not anything like Sonny, is he?"

"No." She thought of his challenging smile and changed her mind. "Well, maybe a little." Then she frowned. "What does Sonny have to do with anything?"

"Most of the men you go for remind me of him."

"The men, as in plural? There haven't been so many."

"That's right," Devlin mused. "Instead of dating around, you just get serious, fast."

Cyndi bristled. "So I'm not casual about it, okay? Is that really a crime?"

After her divorce, it had been more than a year before she'd had more than one date with the same man. Devlin had called her picky. Cyndi hadn't been interested in repeating past mistakes.

Then there had been another serious relationship with a television sportscaster. Cyndi had cared for Tom, but their relationship had become more habit than anything else. It had lacked some elusive quality. Passion, perhaps. Believing that lack her own problem, Cyndi had ended the engagement last year. Devlin had made no secret of his relief. He never thought Tom was the man for her. But Tom hadn't been like Sonny. Handsome, yes. And popular with everyone, but...

Devlin broke into her thoughts. "The men you like are always a little too smooth. Nick seems a little rougher around the edges."

The memory of Nick's mouth moving across her own made Cyndi smile. "He's smooth enough."

"Oh, yeah?" Devlin smiled. "You've got that dreamy look in your eyes, Sis."

Grabbing a sponge from the back of the sink, Cyndi put extra force into wiping off the table. "The only thing in my eyes is weariness. It's late."

"Okay, okay," her brother said. "I'm only going to offer one parting piece of advice."

"Which I will take to heart, of course," she joked.

"Seriously..."

Cyndi turned, surprised by the gravity of his tone. "What is it?"

"Don't question everything," he said. "Go away with Nick tomorrow and the next day and the day after that if you want. And just have fun, Cyndi. Promise me you'll do that. Promise you'll stop worrying about past mistakes long enough to enjoy today."

His perception astounded her. "You've really got me all figured out, don't you?"

Devlin's blue eyes again flashed with teasing lights. "Haven't I told you before that I know everything?"

They had laughed. Easy, familiar laughter. But his words had stuck with Cyndi. She held on to them now as the boat approached Catalina. The wind was cooler here, making her glad she had chosen white slacks and put a jacket over her loose, tangerine-colored sweater. On impulse, she snuggled closer to Nick's side, earning a glance from him.

"I'm really glad I came," she said.

"So am I." He turned to study the shoreline. "Have you ever been here?"

Cyndi nodded. "Years ago. You?"

"Are you kidding? Since coming to L.A., the only tourist attraction I've visited is Disneyland. And that was only because one of my sisters was visiting and her kids cried and begged for my company.''

The improbable image of Nick in a set of Mickey Mouse ears made her smile. ''I guess you're not the touristy type. What made you choose this place for the weekend?''

Shrugging, Nick just tucked her arm through his. He wasn't about to tell Cyndi that asking her anywhere for the weekend had been pure impulse. As they had sat talking last night, he had known he wanted to be with her this weekend, all weekend. A trip had seemed the answer. Catalina had come to mind because Harris Fielding's wife had told him about a bed-and-breakfast inn owned by some friends. After leaving Cyndi last night, Nick had gone straight to a phone and started calling. Some pleading and manipulation had helped him secure two rooms in that very same inn. He only hoped it lived up to the description Harris's wife had given him.

As it turned out, she hadn't done the place justice.

Tucked behind a low stone wall, the two-story stuccoed residence was surrounded by a tiled courtyard. Water splashed in a small fountain, the spray blowing in the brisk, salty breeze. Gnarled trees made intricate shadows against walls the color of heavy cream.

Inside, the inn was a cozy mix of styles and colors. The owners, an older couple who had lived on the island for years, occupied most of the first floor. Upstairs were four guest rooms, each furnished in comfortable, casual fashion, with family antiques mingling with newer pieces. Nick and Cyndi's rooms were separated by a bathroom but shared a balcony with a stunning view of sky and sea and the dozens of boats cruising toward the island.

As they stood on the balcony before going in search of lunch, Cyndi said, "For someone who doesn't profess to know much about touristy places, you did a good job picking this inn."

Nick only smiled. The impulse and the late-night phone calls had been worth it, if only to see her pleasure. "Let's eat and go exploring."

Following their innkeeper's recommendations, they lunched on shrimp and pasta in a crowded restaurant where picture windows faced the sea. Then they wandered hand in hand through the town of Avalon's quaint streets. Nick was soon laden with packages. Cyndi found something intriguing in every shop—a coral pin for Lin, a fishing hat for her father, lace-edged pillowcases and crystal earrings for herself. For Devlin, she found a silly doctor figurine made from aluminum cans.

While the clerk wrapped the monstrosity in tissue paper, Nick whispered to Cyndi, "Poor Devlin."

"He'll like it because it's ecologically sound. You know—recycled art."

Indeed, everything in the shop had an environmental slant. Sculptures made of discarded plastics. Jewelry designed from fragments of metal and broken glass. Upon handing Cyndi the package, the clerk, instead of thanking her, said, "Love the earth." Cyndi was charmed. Nick pulled her out in the street before she could buy napkin rings fashioned from aluminum pull tabs.

And before they took up their wandering again, he kissed her. Just because she was laughing and the sun was in her hair. Because he feared he was falling in love.

Fear and love. He wondered if those two emotions would always be linked in his mind. It hadn't been that way in the beginning. The first time he had thought himself in love, he hadn't been afraid. He had been all of seventeen. She was a neighborhood girl, a childhood friend who had blossomed into a beauty while his back was turned. For four or five months she had been his—body and soul. Even now he could remember those hot, still nights. The promises in the dark. The shared dreams. For her sake, he even reconsidered his plans to move to New York. Then she had dumped him for an older guy who had marriage, not television, on his mind.

Without love to tie him to the old neighborhood, Nick had gone in pursuit of his dreams. And the next time he loved, he hadn't been quite so free with himself. Little by little, down through the years, he learned to hold back, to be afraid of what love would bring.

Yet here he was. Falling for a woman he didn't understand, who sometimes looked at him with eyes full of distrust. As he followed Cyndi inside still another shop, he wondered at his nerve. Loving Cyndi could be the worst heartbreak of all.

Just slow down, he cautioned himself. Yet that argument didn't wash later that night, when he held Cyndi in his arms on the dance floor of a crowded restaurant. The night was cold enough for a blaze in the big stone fireplace. The music from the live band was muted, romantic. So was the lighting. If they hadn't danced, Nick knew he would have had to find another reason to touch her. But touching her was also a torture all its own.

Cheek pressed to Cyndi's soft hair, he breathed in her fragrance and promptly stumbled. "Sorry," he whispered. "I haven't danced in a while."

Her sigh sounded like contentment. "I guess you could say I dance all the time, coming up with new workout routines. But not like this." Her hand squeezed his slightly. "I'm having a great time."

The movement of her body against his made Nick stumble once more. "Sorry. As my sisters would attest, I've never been much of a dancer, even when I was in practice."

"Your sisters?"

"They tried out their techniques on me. When I balked, Mama would tell me all the practice would come in handy someday."

"And did it?"

He grinned. "I recall being thankful along about the eighth grade when I got to slow dance with Mary Macelli."

"The prettiest girl in school?"

"The most developed, anyway."

"That's terrible," Cyndi admonished.

"Nope, that's a thirteen-year-old boy for you."

She laughed and Nick took a chance on a more intricate step.

"You lied," she said breathlessly, shaking the hair away from her face. "You're a very good dancer."

"It comes with the partner."

For a moment they simply stared into each other's eyes. Cyndi, as usual, was the first to glance away. She wasn't sure where this lovely, enchanted day was leading. She almost didn't care. But just almost.

"How about you?" Nick asked softly. "I don't guess you missed many dances in school."

"I did okay."

"Now, don't be modest. I'm sure they lined up far ahead of time to get a date with you. Everyone wants a date with the prom queen."

"For your information, we didn't have a prom queen."

"So it was homecoming queen, right?"

"Well...yes," Cyndi admitted, flushing. "But most people have it all wrong. Just because everyone thinks you're pretty and votes you an honor like that doesn't mean guys ask you out."

"Oh, right. I'm sure you sat home, dateless all through high school."

"I didn't say that either."

"So there was one special guy?"

Sonny. Odd how her past intruded, though she tried her best to forget.

"Uh-oh," Nick murmured. "Bad memories?"

She nodded, but said nothing. Even considering all she had divulged to Nick last night, she still couldn't tell him about Sonny. A failed marriage was one thing to have on your conscience.

Someone's death was another type of guilt entirely.

"High school." Nick sighed and shook his head. "It seems a million years ago, but it's strange how all the bad stuff that happens sticks with you."

"Yes, strange," Cyndi echoed, without enthusiasm.

"I can still remember standing in the hall at school, in this one particular spot where all the really 'cool' guys stood, hoping that one special girl would smile at me. The wrong one always did."

Cyndi nodded, only half listening to Nick. She could remember Sonny and Ryder and a host of other boys leaning with such careful negligence against lockers, watching the girls go by. She had always gotten her share of whistles and been secretly pleased when Sonny would shush his friends and stake his claim by leaving them to walk her down the hall.

Actually she had enjoyed the whistles, too. It had seemed like such innocent fun. But on prom night, when Sonny told her every guy in school had the hots for her, her perception of that male appreciation had changed. Those remembered whistles had stopped seeming so innocent. Cyndi had never walked past a group of guys with the same sort of confidence again.

Now, as the tempo of the song changed, she suggested to Nick, "Let's sit this one out."

He nodded, but as they threaded their way across the crowded dance floor on the way to their table, a woman stopped them. "You are Cyndi Saint, aren't you?" she asked when Cyndi gave her a puzzled look. "I love your exercise program."

Pleased yet somewhat embarrassed by the recognition, Cyndi chatted with the woman for a moment before going on her way. At the table, she asked Nick if they could leave and walk back to the inn. She was tired, and the warm, smoky room was getting to her.

Outside, the wind was blowing hard off the ocean. Most of the people who had crowded the street during the day were inside, out of the cold. Cyndi wished she had left on her slacks instead of changing into a denim skirt and matching top for dinner. Shivering, she paused outside the restaurant door and buttoned her jacket.

"Sure you want to walk?" Nick asked.

"It's cold, but in a way it feels good."

"Did getting recognized back there feel good, too?"

She laughed. "That doesn't happen often, but when it does, I feel kind of weird."

He tucked her arm through his as they turned toward the waterfront. "You're something else, Cyndi Saint."

"What do you mean?"

"I just don't know too many celebrities—"

Her laughter cut him off. "I'm a far cry from that. Like I said, getting recognized happens infrequently."

"But most people would get a charge out of it. I knew this woman . . ." He paused but then continued, "This woman was a newscaster, a popular one, on a leading New York television channel. Her face was on billboards, in newspaper ads, plastered all over the city. She got really caught up in her own celebrity. It was her whole life. It got so we couldn't go to dinner without being interrupted." Bitterness crept into his voice. "She loved the attention."

"And you hated it," Cyndi murmured. His use of "we" had told her this woman had been special to him, perhaps the same one who had taught him to keep his work and personal life separate.

Beneath a street lamp Nick drew to a halt, his gaze turning toward the darkened sea. "I didn't hate that Nancy was successful, or even that she was recognized," he muttered. "But I hated how much it all meant to her."

"It drove you apart?"

His mouth twisted. "You could say that. We broke up when I was no longer useful. After I left her newscast, which I produced, and took another job, she took another lover. Job security, you know."

So now Cyndi understood his fears about business and pleasure. "Nancy sounds very insecure."

His laugh was short. "Maybe, though I doubt it. What she was was plastic. Cold, hard plastic. After she betrayed me, I realized the little bit of warmth she showed me was all an act."

And Nick Calderaro wouldn't want a woman who was anything less than honest. That's what he was—an honest, real, what-you-see-is-what-you-get kind of guy. He wanted the same kind of woman, someone who could face him with confidence and strength. The only way a woman would survive with a man like him was to be just as strong as he was.

Cyndi didn't know if she was up to the challenge. Perhaps the better question was whether she wanted the challenge. Did she want Nick Calderaro?

The thought made her dizzy. This was all so fast. Three days ago, she and Nick had merely been co-workers. More adversaries than anything, really, with only a vague sort of attraction between them. Now she was standing at his side, wondering if she could be the sort of woman he needed and wanted. As if she had ever been the kind of woman any man needed. In the past...

The past was exactly what she wasn't supposed to be thinking of this weekend. *Enjoy today.* Devlin's words came back, stiffening her resolve to resist her memories.

"Cyndi?" Nick said, and captured her attention again as he drew her closer to his side. In the light that spilled from the streetlight, his eyes were dark with some emotion she couldn't name. "I thought you were like Nancy at first," he said. "Just another ambitious bitch."

"You've changed your mind?"

Drawing a hand through her hair, he smiled. "Isn't that obvious?"

She let her breath escape and forced a shaky smile. "I've never been ambitious."

He laughed. "That's not the sort of thing a person usually admits to their boss."

"You're forgetting you're not my boss during my off time."

"A momentary lapse," he said, smiling. "But I still don't understand the lack of ambition. In a few weeks a national cablevision show will debut with you as host. It's your second show. If you're not ambitious, how did you get to this point?"

"Luck, I guess," Cyndi admitted. "I was lucky six years ago when a reporter took my exercise class and convinced her boss to put me on the air. Then I was lucky enough to work with talented people. Lucky that the network spotted me and hired Lin to direct my show.''

''People spend their entire lives trying to make that kind of luck happen.''

She frowned. ''I know. Sometimes I feel I don't deserve anything that's happened.''

''What do you want to happen next?''

''I just want to get through each day of this new show.''

''You'll do it,'' Nick said. ''Keep trying. Don't let down your guard like you did yesterday.''

Groaning, Cyndi pulled away from him. ''I don't want to think about yesterday. I don't want to think about the show at all.'' Sighing, she shook her head. ''But that's not entirely true—I do want it to be successful.''

''Sounds like ambition to me.''

''It's fear. Simple fear of the unknown. Part of me is scared to death for the show to go on the air. The other part just wants to have it over with, to know how it will be received. I'd be content with a long-running show, some genuine security.''

He laughed. ''Which is exactly what every person in television wants.''

''I know, I know,'' she said. ''But some people actually enjoy the uncertainty. I hate it. Some nights I drive home from the studio just wishing I could look up in the sky and see exactly what the stars have in store for me.''

''Don't tell me you believe that stuff.''

Cyndi glanced up. "Just look at that sky and tell me there's not some kind of magic at work. Otherwise, how could it be so beautiful?"

"Yes," Nick murmured, his hand lifting to her cheek. "So beautiful."

She looked at him and realized his compliment was for her, not the sky. Then his lips danced across hers. Lightly. In much the same way as he had kissed her several times today. But differently, too. It wasn't like the hot, demanding kiss they had shared last night. This kiss was warm, filled with promise. The promise of what, Cyndi wasn't sure. The kiss shook her. At the same time, it left her with a strange sense of calm. Lord, but this man confused her. The only thing she was certain of was her desire to understand him.

Nick drew away, taking her hand, and with heads ducked against the ever-increasing wind, they struggled back to the inn. Brandy, hot tea and coffee were waiting in the many-windowed room that faced the courtyard. After the cold night, the cozy room, with its dim lights and plump-cushioned seats, was a welcome respite.

Their hosts soon retired, and the other guests didn't appear, leaving Cyndi and Nick to enjoy their solitude. The windows rattled and trees scratched against the walls outside, but they were more than content inside. Cyndi snuggled into one corner of the sofa, while Nick sat with both legs outstretched in front of him. And they talked. For hours. About books and television, politics and religion. They argued, laughed and opened up to each other.

It was a special night. An intimate night. So perfect, Cyndi felt only regret when the grandfather clock in the corner chimed two. Reluctantly she climbed the stairs beside Nick. Outside her door, she stood, feeling uncertain, wondering what might happen next. Would Nick make some move? How would she react?

But all he did was squeeze her hand and go to his own room, leaving her with no choice but to bid him good-night. In her room, she stood, back to the door, feeling foolish, yearning for the courage to suggest they not spend this night alone.

She could imagine the way he would react. How his dark eyebrows might draw together. The lines that would frame his mouth if he smiled. The way his hands—those broad boxer's hands—would feel on her skin. Rough and tender. Like his kiss. A kiss that would taste of brandy and coffee. He would touch her with care. And urgency. She could feel his touch. On her breasts. Her thighs. Between them.

Stifling a cry, Cyndi pushed away from the door. She was being silly. Nick was in the other room, and it was doubtful she would work up enough nerve to do any of the things she imagined. Even if she had the nerve, it wouldn't be the way she dreamed. It never was.

Yet the fantasies continued. Once in bed, Cyndi tossed and turned, trying to put Nick and his disturbing proximity out of her thoughts. Finally, in frustration, she threw back her covers and headed for the French doors that opened onto the balcony. Maybe some fresh air would cool her overactive imagination. Her hand was on the doorknob when she glanced

through the sheer curtains. Nick was outside. Silhou-
etted in a pool of light from his own room, he stood
with hands braced on the railing, looking out at the
sea. It took only a second for Cyndi to see that he was
naked. Completely, gloriously naked.

Heart thudding, she shrank against the wall. She
didn't breathe for fear Nick would turn and see her.
Yet she couldn't stop herself from peering out at him
again. He hadn't moved, and she grew bold enough to
push the curtain away from a corner of the window.
His back was muscular. Like his legs. And his trim
derriere.

And he had to be freezing to death.

Stepping carefully back from the door, Cyndi began to smile. Perhaps Nick was standing in the cold
wind for the very reason she had been about to go
outside. Because he needed to get something—or
someone—off his mind before he could sleep.

And perhaps that someone was her.

That was assuming a lot, considering he hadn't even
kissed her good-night. But the possibility was exciting.

The excitement was still there when she awoke. It
was just beneath the surface all the next day while she
and Nick finished exploring the island and caught the
boat for home.

She knew what she needed to do was get away from
him, go where she could think without the distraction
brought by his presence. But she was also reluctant for
their weekend to end. When he suggested dinner at his
place, she foolishly agreed. They shopped and headed

for his apartment, even though tension, like wire on a spool, wrapped tighter and tighter around Cyndi.

At his place, Nick dropped his overnight bag to the foyer's slate floor and stepped aside to allow Cyndi to enter. "Enter at your own risk. My cleaning service decided to go out of business last week."

Carrying a grocery bag, Cyndi preceded him down the three steps to the living area. "I'm sure it's not that bad."

"I'm usually pretty neat." Nick plucked a discarded shirt and tie from the back of his favorite leather chair. They joined a pile of similar garments on the railing of the stairs leading to his loft bedroom before he took the grocery bag from Cyndi. "I just haven't had time to hire a new service. You know how hectic it's been."

"Of course," Cyndi said, dropping her purse to the chair. She turned to study the room. His apartment building was only blocks from the ocean, much closer than hers to the place where they had caught the boat for Catalina. So for convenience's sake, she had met him here Saturday morning, but she hadn't come inside. The apartment seemed right for Nick—lots of open space, clean lines, wood and leather upholstery.

Nick tried to view his home as she might see it. This room was large, open to the loft above, with a skylight centered over the living area. The floors were pine planked, covered in places with rugs of deep charcoal. Magazines and newspapers littered the low marble-topped table in front of a sofa grouping. Videotapes overflowed the shelves beside his widescreen television. In the window-lined alcove that he used as an office, his desk was buried under a mass of computer printouts.

Shifting the groceries from one arm to the other, Nick gave Cyndi a sheepish smile. "I guess the place is a wreck."

Again her gaze swept through the room. "I like it," she said finally.

"You're an easy lady to please, Miss Saint." He started toward the kitchen-dining area at the other end of the room. "Come make yourself at home up here. I know I left the kitchen in pretty good shape." After depositing the bag of groceries on the butcher block in the center of the kitchen, he moved from window to window, opening blinds. Late-afternoon sunlight filled the room with mellow light.

Cyndi paused at the window behind the dining table. "Looks like we're going to have another spectacular sunset."

From over her shoulder, Nick studied the orange globe of the sun, poised over the ocean in the distance. "A fitting end to a spectacular weekend," he murmured, stepping forward to slip his arms around Cyndi's waist.

She hesitated only slightly before folding her hands over his and leaning back. Nick closed his eyes and savored the feel of her in his arms. After the wanting had robbed him of sleep last night, he had wanted her all day today. He couldn't remember now when he hadn't wanted Cyndi. In his home. In his embrace. In his bed.

That image brought the expected tightening of his body. Turning his head, he pressed a kiss to the skin just below her ear. His tongue moved softly across her flesh. She drew a quick breath, and he felt the shudder that ran through her body.

But she moved away. "You promised me dinner, didn't you?"

He regarded her silently. She was looking everywhere but at him, picking up pewter candlesticks from the sideboard, studying a group of family photographs on the wall above it. When she at last glanced up, her smile—the one he thought of as her public smile—was firmly in place.

"And some wine, too," she prompted. Her laughter was bright, artificial sounding. "You bought my favorite, remember?"

Nick nodded and moved into the kitchen. While he rummaged in a drawer for the corkscrew and poured her a glass of wine, Cyndi kept up a running dialogue about everything and nothing in particular. The nonstop chatter told him she was nervous. He just wasn't sure why.

Finally, when even the wine didn't relax her, he turned from the grocery bag he was unpacking and cut her off in midsentence. "Is there something wrong, Cyndi?"

"Of course not," she answered. But once again her smile was too bright, too impersonal.

"Then what's with the act?"

"I don't know what you mean."

"Yes, you do."

"I guess I'm tired."

She started to turn away from him, but Nick took her arm. "If you didn't want to come over here, you didn't have to, you know."

"But I wanted to," she protested, giving him a weak smile. "You promised me a big steak and salad with herb dressing, the kind your mother—"

"And that's the only reason you came here?"

She paused, a brief lapse that seemed to stretch forever between them. Yet, finally, she raised blue eyes full of confusion to meet his gaze. "I guess I don't know why I'm here," she whispered. "I'll go—"

"No." Hands moving to her shoulders, he held her steady in front of him. "I don't want you to leave. Please." He hadn't meant to sound desperate. Desperation wasn't his style in dealing with women, any woman, even Cyndi, who was different from any woman he had ever known. But he couldn't seem to stop himself. "Please—"

She kissed him then, catching him off guard. Tenderly, with infinite care, her mouth moved and opened against his. But Nick soon took what she offered and made it his own, letting the caress grow and change, become insistent. They kissed until his desire was a stinging, hardening demand. Lost in her scent, in the soft cries she made against his mouth, he slipped his hands to her hips and pulled her tight against him.

"This is why you came here," he whispered. He kissed her again. "We've fought this all weekend. But it's what you want, isn't it?" He didn't pause for her answer. "It's what I want, Cyndi. God, I want you so much. The same as you want me."

"Nick, I don't know—"

"You can tell me what you want."

"No, I—"

"Tell me," he murmured before trailing kisses up her neck. Her chin went up, her neck arching. He felt the muscles working in her throat. "Tell me what pleases you, Cyndi. You can tell me."

"But I can't," she said, her voice breaking. "I can't, Nick."

Realizing she had become still in his arms, Nick drew back. "Cyndi? Cyndi, what's wrong?"

She stepped away. "I can't," she said. "I just . . . can't."

Puzzled by her reaction, Nick frowned. "Can't tell me?" He reached for her hand. She retreated again. "Cyndi, honey, what's wrong?"

Instead of answering, she shook her head and started for the living room. "I'm sorry," she whispered. "I'm not trying to be a tease, truly I'm not. . . ."

"Then stay here," he said, following her. "Tell me what I did, what I said."

"It isn't you," she cried, grabbing her purse from his chair. "Don't you understand? It's me."

"I don't know what you mean."

"I'm sorry," Cyndi said once more.

Nick followed her to the door, asking her again and again to tell him what was wrong. But without a backward glance, she left him standing.

His entreaties were still ringing in Cyndi's ears when she got in her car. Shame made her face burn as she drove toward the Coast, into the last, dying rays of the weekend's sunshine.

So here she was, running away again. But not because she was frightened of what Nick had been offering her. But because she wasn't. She hadn't left because she didn't want him. She did. With wild, almost unrecognizable yearning, she wanted him. And that was the hardest thing of all to face. With Nick, all the feelings she had buried with Sonny had been resurrected. Nick made her ache. He made her want. He made her believe she had something to offer a man. He made her think passion was more than a schoolgirl's forgotten dream.

Down deep inside Cyndi, the part of her self she had believed dead, was coming back to life. But she didn't know what to do with those feelings. She couldn't quite trust them.

And so she kept driving. She turned up the Coast, as usual. Even though there was a part of her that wanted to turn around and go back to Nick, she didn't. It was safer to keep running.

Chapter Seven

Nick had seldom run from challenges. In his personal and professional life he had faced tough decisions. On occasion, he had made bad choices and lived with the consequences. He knew how it felt to fail. He also knew the peculiar, sometimes unexpected pressures of success. He wasn't a coward.

Yet he had never dreaded anything the way he dreaded seeing Cyndi again. In fact, he avoided her for three days.

Why had she run away? After the weekend they had shared, with the feeling of closeness that had grown between them, the last thing he had expected was for her to leave so abruptly and in such an agitated state. Again and again he replayed their last moments together. He didn't know what he had done wrong. If he remembered correctly, Cyndi had kissed him.

Yes, that memory was clear—the sweet, giving pressure of her mouth against his. Discarding any pretense of work, Nick rocked back in his desk chair, finger tapping against his lips as he thought of Cyndi's kiss. Even now her taste was still with him. As was the stricken look that had been in her blue eyes when she left.

What had happened?

The buzz of the phone made him scowl. He snatched up the receiver, barking his name so that his secretary paused a second before telling him Lin Redding was waiting outside to see him. Smoothing his tie as he replaced the phone, Nick stood just as Lin walked in his door.

As was her way, she wasted no time on preliminaries. "You haven't been down to the studio this week."

Nick offered her a seat and ignored the question her statement implied. He turned to the small wet bar that seemed to be standard issue in television executives' offices. "Coffee, cola, mineral water?"

"I wanted to know if something was going on that I needed to be told about."

He emptied his second pot of coffee for the day. His caffeine consumption was reaching new proportions. "Nothing's wrong," he said, turning from the bar with a steaming mug in hand. "I've been busy, and you and Joe—"

"Are doing a bang-up job," Lin completed, perching on the edge of her chair like a bird about to take flight. "I know that, and I know you know it. But I still thought you would be on the set through these first few weeks of tapings. I was half-afraid you were already bored with this place and were leaving."

"My reputation for abrupt departures is bothering you, is it?"

"I don't want you to leave."

"Thanks for the vote of confidence. I'm not thinking of leaving." He grinned. "Not yet, anyway."

Lin sat back in her chair. "That's good to hear."

Nick took a seat at his desk and gestured to the paperwork spread in front of him. "As you can see, I've got a lot of things going."

"And the network has invested a lot of hopes in our show. I thought you'd be around more."

"I'm confused," he said, leaning forward. "Most people would like having a free hand, not having the network brass breathing down their necks."

"Oh, Nick." Lin shoved a hand through her dark hair, pulling several strands free of the kelly green barrette that matched her short-skirted suit. "You're not one of the brass," she said. "I don't think of you as the big boss who's going to lower the boom on us at any minute. You really understand what it's like to pull a show like this together. I welcome your input. So do Joe and everyone else who's involved in the show. Otherwise, I certainly wouldn't be up here asking where you've been all week."

"You're not having problems, are you?"

"No, and I don't expect any."

Nick shuffled some papers before asking, as casually as possible, the question that was most on his mind. "So how's Cyndi doing?"

"Fine. She came back kind of weirded out after the weekend—"

He glanced up, but nothing in Lin's expression revealed she knew where and with whom Cyndi had spent the weekend.

"But I thought that might be normal considering what happened on Friday."

"Friday?"

"The interview," Lin prompted. "Cyndi's terrible interview. Which, by the way, came out beautifully after editing. You ought to stop by and see it."

"I'll do that," Nick promised absently, and cut back to Cyndi. "She's okay now, isn't she? Not... uh...weirded out."

"No," Lin said, then paused. "Any special reason you want to know?"

Gazing into her green-brown eyes, Nick knew he wasn't fooling her at all. It would take someone with their emotions more under control than his to fool a woman this shrewd. He sat back in his chair. "There's a lot I'd like to know about Cyndi."

Lin's smile was smug.

"What's that look for?"

"It's just that I knew there was something happening between the two of you. I wasn't completely sure until now and Cyndi hasn't said a word, of course, but—"

"She doesn't confide in you?"

"About some things, but she's a very private person."

"Tell me about it," Nick muttered. "I spent the entire weekend trying to figure her out."

"So you're the reason she came in Monday looking like hell."

He frowned. "She looked like hell?" Remorse, like an ache, squeezed through his chest, although he still didn't know what he had done to so upset Cyndi. Swearing softly, he shoved away from his desk and turned to the view from his window. Only it was Cyndi's face, not the office buildings, that he saw.

"Don't be so hard on yourself," Lin said.

"I feel as if I hurt her, but I didn't intend to. And I don't know how or why it happened."

"She isn't easy to understand."

He turned around. "But you understand her, right?"

Lin shrugged. "Sometimes I think I do. Then other times, I don't think anyone, not her brother, whom she's closest to, or even Cyndi herself, can understand her."

"So it's not easy being her friend."

"Not easy but worth it. Maybe I try harder because she and I are a lot alike."

Over the past few weeks he had often thought Lin and Cyndi were unlikely friends because of their differences. Lin was assertive, a bit brash, a lot bold. "I don't see the similarities," he said now.

Lin laughed. "It's exactly what you *see* that makes us similar. It isn't easy to always be judged by what's on the outside, Nick. That's what Cyndi and I have in common. She's beautiful, and I'm different. Most people never get past our exteriors."

Remembering what Cyndi had told him about Lin's background, he studied the woman in front of him.

Her face—the color of her eyes, their shape, the molding of her features—was a blend of two races. The mix had given her an exotic beauty, but it had sometimes placed her in two worlds. So much conflict over such superficial differences. He couldn't understand why that mattered so much to some people.

"I don't think like most people," he told Lin. "I look below the surface. The fact that Cyndi is beautiful doesn't mean as much to me as getting to know the person inside."

"Then you'll have to dig. People like Cyndi and I, we get used to nobody caring what's inside." She laughed. "Now some, like me, grow up shouting for attention, making ourselves heard. Others, like Cyndi, learn to hide. They try to make sure what's inside is just as picture perfect as what's outside. You and I know that's never the case, but they hide what could be seen as imperfections."

"She doesn't let anyone close enough to see inside."

Lin nodded. "So no one can disapprove of what they see. That way she doesn't get hurt nearly as often."

Nick lowered himself into his chair. "I think I'm beginning to understand just what I'm up against."

"She would be worth the struggle," Lin said softly. "I'm even willing to go out on a limb and say you might be awfully good for her."

Nick shot her a grin. "How kind of you, Miss Redding."

She got to her feet. ''Now, are you going to start coming around or what? We're shooting on location the rest of this week. I sure wouldn't mind getting your perspective.''

''You can count on me, Lin. Just tell me when and where.''

The when was early the next morning. The where was one of Beverly Hills's most exclusive beauty salons. Two women—average, yet attractive women in their early thirties—were being treated to make-overs. While the tape rolled, Cyndi was to chat with the stylists and emphasize beauty tips that viewers could apply to themselves. The made-over women would come back to the studio after they were finished to do a wrap-up with her. It was a day-long project, which would eventually be only ten or fifteen minutes when the program aired.

The subject matter didn't interest Nick in the least. But he knew it was perfect for the show's target audience. He also knew how Joe and Lin planned to lift the segment from the ordinary by turning it into a slick little storybook fable. With music, graphics and Cyndi's charm, they shouldn't have any trouble.

And Cyndi was charming. Poised, warm and personable, she put her two guests at ease. She was using everything she had learned. She even suggested a change in camera angle on an important shot. It worked. She worked.

And she left Nick feeling dizzy.

By midmorning, he was wondering why he had come. Except for making a few suggestions at the outset, he wasn't helping anyone. Lin had simply been feeling the pressure yesterday when she asked him to join them on the shoot. The only reason he had for hanging around was to be near Cyndi. Yet that was foolish. There were several opportunities for her to break the deep-freeze treatment she was giving him, but she didn't. She talked to him, yes. She was polite. She smiled. Like a windup doll, she went through all the paces. That made him angrier than if she had ignored him altogether.

So, finally, he left.

He went back to his office, where there were decisions to be made and proposals to be read. He put Cyndi out of his mind. Lin might have given him some insight into Cyndi's character, but that didn't mean he had to be the one who crawled to her. Nick Calderaro had never crawled for anyone, ever. He vowed he wouldn't start now.

It was after nine that night when he gave in.

As he walked up the sidewalk to Cyndi's front door, he told himself he wasn't crawling. He just wanted some answers. Something had started between them, and after brushing him off Sunday night, she owed him an explanation. He put four days' worth of anger and frustration into his touch on the doorbell.

Cyndi finally opened the door on the bell's fourth ring. She was belting a floral robe that looked like silk. Her hair was mussed, her expression dazed. There was a red spot on her cheek, as if it had most recently been snuggled up against a pillow.

"You were sleeping," Nick said, although that was nothing like what he had intended to say to her. "I'm sorry. I thought you'd be up."

"It was a long day." Pointedly, or so he thought, she didn't open the door wider or invite him in.

"I know you're tired. But we have to talk."

"You really want to talk to me?"

He swore briefly, profanely, rather pleased when Cyndi fell back a step. "Would I have driven all the way out here if I didn't *really* want to talk?"

Blue eyes widening, she swung the door open and stepped aside.

"Is your brother here?" Nick asked as he strode into her living room. Cyndi shook her head. "Good. I don't want to be interrupted. I also don't want you running away."

Near the middle of the room, he turned to face her. Cyndi paused behind one of the couches, gripping the soft cushions as if they were a shield. She looked frightened, and that wasn't what he wanted.

"I'm not doing this right," Nick muttered, loosening his tie. "I knew I wouldn't do this right. That's why I didn't follow you Sunday night. That's why every time I reached for the phone, I stopped myself."

"I know," Cyndi whispered. "I almost called you, too."

"Why didn't you?"

"I didn't know what to say."

Because what he wanted to do was put his arms around her, Nick shoved his hands into his pockets. "Just explain to me. Tell me why you left Sunday."

Her hands dug deeper into the cushion. "It just wasn't...right."

He stepped toward her. "What wasn't right? Kissing me? Why wouldn't that be right?"

"You don't understand."

"Make me."

She bit her lip and looked away.

Frustrated, Nick spread his hands wide. "Talk to me, Cyndi. I'll never understand unless you talk. And I'm telling you now, I'm not just going to walk out that door and be satisfied that you can't explain things to me. We aren't playing games—"

"Everyone's always accusing me of that," she protested. "I'm not playing, Nick. I don't like games any more than you do."

"Then be straight with me."

"I am being straight. I don't completely understand why I had to run away. But I knew I just couldn't handle it...you...or me...." She faltered.

He shook his head. "What do you think, Cyndi, that I was going to force you into something you didn't want?"

"Of course not—"

"But that's how it sounds." Anger started curling through his gut once more. What did she take him for? "I'm not in the habit of forcing women. If you had said no, that would have been enough. I don't think no means yes. That's not the kind of man I am. You know that. You know me better than that."

Cyndi whirled away from the couch, arms folded across her middle as she paced toward the fireplace. "But that's just the point, Nick. I really don't know you. We had this . . . thing going between us and we went away and we had a nice time. But I wasn't ready for anything more.''

"What did I ask for?" Nick demanded. "You kissed me, remember? And that's all it was. A kiss. An innocent kiss."

"There was nothing innocent about it."

"No," he muttered, closing the distance between them with broad strides. "You're right. It wasn't innocent. Just as there's not anything tame or simple about the way you make me feel, Cyndi. If there were I wouldn't be here now, burying my pride. I would have written you off as a cold, manipulative bitch."

She spun to face him again. "That's what you men always want to believe, isn't it? When a woman doesn't respond the way you want, you say she's cold and you walk away."

"I didn't walk," Nick reminded her, his voice soft. He reached out, smoothing a tendril of hair from her cheek. "You did."

She jerked away from his touch. "Maybe I didn't like the way you responded."

Before she could retreat behind another piece of furniture, Nick captured her hands in his. "You're a terrible liar, Cyndi. I was there, remember? I know there was something special happening between us this weekend. Why did that scare you so?"

Cyndi closed her eyes. For three long, dreadful days she had wondered how she would react to Nick when she saw him again. And then today, when he had shown up at the shoot, she hadn't known what to say or do. There had been too many people around for a truly personal conversation, but she had seen Nick wanted something from her. He had stood there, his face stony and full of hurt. It seemed every time she looked up, he was watching her, waiting for the explanation she knew she owed him.

Opening her eyes, she whispered, "Sometimes I wish you hadn't walked into my life, Nick Calderaro. You complicate everything."

"You can't live, *really* live without complications."

She thought of her mother, who Devlin had said never knew the real, gritty facts of life. It was a certainty Fran Saint had never run into a complication like Nick.

"It doesn't matter what you wish," he said, "because I'm here and this is where I want to be."

"You'd regret it."

His expression changing, softening, he drew her close. "I'll tell you what I regret," he whispered. "I regret the last few days and my not having enough courage to track you down, to make you talk to me. I regret every minute I'm not with you, every night we don't spend together."

Cyndi shook her head. She wanted to stay right here in Nick's arms. She wanted to believe all the sweet, tender things he was saying. She wanted to think that with him it would be different. But she still couldn't believe that. Growing closer to him wouldn't be wise. Because she wanted him, because he made her feel ripe with yearning, what he offered her was too much of a risk. If she failed Nick, as she had failed so many times, she knew her heart would never stop breaking.

The load she carried was already too heavy; she couldn't add to it.

So she pushed him away. "This isn't what I want."

He took her hand again. "Yes, it is."

"Stop telling me that," she cried, shaking him off. "You don't know me, Nick. I'm no good at this."

"What's to be good at? I care about you."

"You can't know that yet."

He brushed her objection aside with a sweep of his hand. "So it's happening fast, like a runaway train. So what? We should climb aboard and see where the feelings take us."

"No, that's not what I want."

His eyes narrowed, but he looked oddly boyish, with his tie askew and his dark hair curling over his forehead. His smile was a brave attempt that somehow failed. "Come on, Cyndi, help me out here. I mean, I'm laying it on the line with you. I care, all right." His hands went to his chest. "I really care. That's not easy for me to admit."

"Then you shouldn't."

He took half a step forward. "Then what do you want from me?"

"Nothing," she said flatly. "I want nothing from you. In fact, I wish you would go away."

It was painful to watch, the way the hope went out of his eyes. He changed so quickly. One minute he was the ardent suitor of her weekend fantasies. The next he was once more the wary stranger who had regarded her with cynicism.

His voice low, he said, "Do you enjoy this?"

She turned away, unable to stand the hurt in his face. "Why don't you just go, Nick. There's nothing else for us to say to each other."

"But I want to know if you enjoy this. I mean, there are species who make eating their mates part of the whole courting ritual. If you enjoy this it will prove to me exactly what I've been suspecting—that you're not quite human."

Trembling, her heart aching inside her chest, Cyndi started walking. *Run away,* the voice inside her whispered. *Run away again. And don't look back.*

"You can't be real," Nick jeered. "If you were real, you wouldn't have played with me like this. Like I'm some toy for your secret enjoyment. Is that what excites you? Do you get your kicks from twisting people inside out?"

His next words were profane, the same ugly words Sonny had once thrown at her. They hit Cyndi like stones, halting her retreat from the room.

"I pity that poor schmuck you married, you know. Because you couldn't have loved him. You couldn't have loved anyone."

Something inside Cyndi snapped as she turned to face Nick's anger. "You don't know who I've loved," she whispered. "You don't know how I've hurt."

Nick's mouth thinned. "Plastic doesn't bleed, Queenie."

"But I'm not plastic," she protested. "I'm flesh and blood. I have feelings. Men always want to forget that. They want what I offer, but only when it's on their terms. And no matter what I give, it's never enough."

"Oh, and what have you given?"

"Everything." The room seemed to spin as she reached for the back of a chair for support. "They take everything I have. They take who I am. And even that isn't enough. The love turns to hate. And what am I left with?" Her voice broke on a sob. "When it's over, all I have is a grave or house or several wasted years. Just one more thing to feel guilty about, that's what I have."

Dimly she was aware of Nick moving toward her, the anger having fled from his face.

"That's why I can't love you," she murmured through the tears she was battling. "That's why I can't let this go any further, Nick. I can't make love with you. I can't fall in love with you. It won't be right. I know it won't be right."

Through some act of will or coercion—she was never sure which—Nick maneuvered her onto the couch. She kept protesting, telling him to leave, pleading with him to understand why she couldn't love him. He paid no attention. He just held her. He stroked her hair. He allowed her to cry.

The only thing Nick made her do was tell him about Sonny. And once she started talking, the whole tale came tumbling out. Nick had that talent, of making her reveal everything. She let it all out—the way Sonny had rejected her and the way he had died. By the time she reached the end of her story, she had no more tears left to cry.

"I don't know exactly what happened after I left the party that night," she said, trying to remember those fuzzy, pain-filled days following the prom. "If someone told me the details, I don't remember. I know

Sonny got on Ryder's motorcycle. I suppose they were drinking. My father woke me that morning and told me Sonny was dead.''

''He left you with a grave,'' Nick murmured, echoing her words.

Pain tightened around her heart, thinking of Sonny being laid to rest. She remembered the sickening smell of flowers. The way his mother had cried. She recalled looking for Meredith. Perhaps Jennifer had spoken to her. The only memory that was clear was the guilt that had borne down on her. That guilt was with her still.

''It was my fault,'' she said out loud. ''I killed Sonny.''

''What?''

She sat up, withdrawing from Nick's embrace. ''It was all my fault. Sonny was upset about something that night. We all were upset. I don't know what it was. Something in the air, maybe. When you're eighteen it doesn't take much to send you into a tailspin. But if I wasn't going to go through with what I started with him, I shouldn't have started it at all. All I did was make him angry and reckless....''

Nick grasped her shoulders, making her face him again. ''That's nonsense, Cyndi. You know it's crazy. If you weren't ready for that kind of relationship, he shouldn't have used threats to try and force you.'' His expression changed, hardened. ''Although I'm not much better, am I? I came over here to force the issue with you tonight.''

Gently she touched his cheek. ''For sex, Nick? Did you come here for sex?''

"You know that isn't the whole issue—"

"And it wasn't just sex for Sonny, either. It was proof of something. That he was a man, maybe."

"Real men don't have to prove who they are."

"But don't you see, he was just a boy trying to be a man. And I was his girl." A smile touched her lips. How childish the phrase seemed now. But that didn't keep her from saying it, "I was Sonny's girl."

Nick stiffened. "What does Sonny mean to you now?"

"He's been dead for almost ten years."

"But you still believe all those things he said about you, don't you?"

She looked down, studying her hands. "I believe that I loved him," she murmured. "I loved him, but I didn't understand him. I was foolish and young and I didn't know what he needed from me. And in a way, I guess I did play with him. I was afraid he was going to leave me for another girl, so I agreed to make love. It was a selfish motive, I was playing with grown-up fire."

"But awhile ago, you said you gave and gave and got nothing in return. That doesn't sound selfish."

"I was upset, Nick, I don't know what I said."

"And maybe what you said then came from your heart. Maybe it's the truth."

"I let Sonny down," Cyndi insisted. "He wanted one thing from me. And I let him down. I sent him away hurt and angry. And he died. He died because of me."

"He wanted what you weren't ready to give. And then he said you were cold and frigid, incapable of response."

She stood. "I shouldn't have told you that."

"You weren't cold in my arms," Nick said, rising also. "You were anything but cold. That's what scares you, isn't it? The fact that Sonny was wrong. Your poor, tragic, dead hero was wrong. But if you admit how wrong he was, you've betrayed him."

He saw in Cyndi's face that he had struck close to the truth, but she denied it, "You've got it all confused."

"No, you do." With a hand under her chin, he pulled her face up to his. "You didn't bury Sonny. You buried yourself."

She pulled back.

"Kiss me," he implored. "Kiss me and then tell me you don't feel anything. Prove that you're unfeeling, incapable of love."

"I don't have to prove anything to you."

"Because you've proven it with others?"

Her gaze fell again. "Nick . . ."

With hands on her arms, he brought her close once more. Her scent, the fragrance that teased him at odd moments and bedeviled his nights, filled his head. "I'm not like the others. I'm not like your precious Sonny or the men he ruined you for."

"Sonny didn't ruin me."

"Right, because you're not ruined at all. And this is proof," Nick muttered, lowering his mouth to hers.

The kiss was hard, raw. The sensations it roused rocked Nick to the core. It moved Cyndi, too. He felt her response. In the lips she opened for his. In the hands that clutched at his shoulders. He kissed her until she relaxed against him. Then he pushed her robe aside and let his hands roam over the silk gown she wore beneath. Her breasts were warm. The nipples pebbled beneath his rotating palms. Reaching down, he dragged the gown upward, until he felt the smooth skin of her thighs against his touch. Softer was the triangle of lace and satin that covered the juncture of her thighs. Softer still were the cries that rose in Cyndi's throat as his touch grew bolder.

When his name was a broken sigh on her lips, he released her.

"How did that feel?" he whispered. "Like nothing?"

Her eyes were filling with tears as he stepped backward. He hadn't meant to make her cry. "I didn't come here to hurt you, Cyndi." His hand went to her hair. "I never want you to be hurt."

Her voice trembled. "Please, just go."

He nodded. "I'll be back, you know. When you get tired of dancing with a ghost, I'll be here." He walked away but turned back when he reached the doorway to the foyer. "Just don't waste any more years, Cyndi. Sonny's the only one who's dead."

Chapter Eight

Like warm, supple fingers, the water caressed Cyndi. Rolling, bubbling against her naked body, the movement relaxed her muscles as she leaned back in her hot tub. The walled garden off her bedroom was removed from prying eyes. The night air was cool on her face, but steamy heat rose from the surface, flushing her skin. With a sigh of pure pleasure, she closed her eyes. The water's comfort was sensual, tantalizing.

Like Nick's touch.

Her eyes flew open. The tension that had drained from her came back in double strength.

Nick.

Just his name brought a deluge of conflicting memories. She could feel his hands on her body. Seductive as sin, his touch had forced her to respond.

Then he had challenged her. She could still hear him telling her not to dance with a ghost.

Sonny's ghost.

Groaning, Cyndi slid downward until her chin touched the water's surface. It had been two days since her Thursday night confrontation with Nick. Friday, at the studio she had been a bundle of nerves, waiting for him to appear at any moment. But he had stayed away. Though he had told her he would come back, she knew he wasn't going to come running to her door again. The next move, if indeed there would be a move, was hers. But what would she do?

The hot tub's jets hummed softly, the only sound in the still February night. Cyndi didn't normally mind the quiet. But tonight it was eerie. Tonight she felt lonely instead of alone. She couldn't help but think of last Saturday when she and Nick had danced and talked and laughed. If only things could have stayed that simple. Why had they become so complicated, so fast?

"It's my fault," she said out loud. She should have stayed well away from Nick Calderaro. He wasn't a simple man. Hadn't she known from the start he would bring trouble into her life? "I'm such a fool," she murmured.

From the side of the tub, Lolita's plaintive meow sounded like an agreement. The cat, eternally fascinated by water, balanced on the wooden edge that rimmed the tub and dipped one pink-padded paw downward.

"Better watch it," Cyndi warned her pet. "You'll fall in."

But Lolita kept her balance, and the water that dampened her paw was enough to satisfy her curiosity. Licking it, she settled back on her haunches and regarded her mistress with what could only be interpreted as smugness.

"I'd like to see how graceful you'd be if you had to venture very far out of this house. It's a rough world out there, kid. You can drown if you're not careful."

The warning was one Cyndi should have heeded herself. Right now, she felt as if she were drowning. Nick had crashed into her life like a riptide. Now she was caught in the rough waters between what her personal history had taught her and what he demanded.

Did she dance with a ghost? She had repeated the question over and over since Nick had walked away from her. Cyndi believed the answer was no. She didn't love Sonny. He had been a dream, a youthful, perfect dream. She hadn't mourned Sonny for years. Her lingering grief was for the person she had been before Sonny died. So, yes, as Nick had said, she buried part of herself with Sonny. There was no big revelation. Though hearing Nick say it was painful, Cyndi had always known the young part of herself, the part that believed in fairy tales and happy endings and everlasting love had been laid to rest forever the night Sonny died.

For a while, she had gone on searching for love with the other men she had allowed into her life. And she had been disappointed. The failures had proven Sonny was right; she was incapable of genuine warmth, of real love. After her relationship with Tom ended last year, she told herself love and passion just weren't meant for her.

Cyndi had very specific dreams about love and passion, dreams she had clung to for years. Love was the heavy perfume of roses, opened wide and shedding their blossoms on a table beside a tumble-sheeted bed. Love could be found in the catch of a voice, in the look that passed between an elderly couple waiting for a bus. Passion was drama. The celluloid sparks between Bogart and Bergman in *Casablanca*. The woman down the street who met her husband in the driveway with a baby on her hip and a kiss that went on forever.

For Cyndi, love and passion were merely images, fuzzy edged, like scenes shot through a gauze-draped lens. She cherished her romantic dreams. They had little to do with the sharp, cutting emotions Nick aroused.

As she had already admitted to herself, Nick had brought something within her back to life. He made her feel. He made her want. What he stirred in her was akin to those tentative, barely blossoming emotions she had known so many years ago, when the rigid, unbreakable rules of her mother had helped her resist the sexual temptation Sonny offered. Yet there was a difference with Nick. The feelings were keener. The want came harder.

It was the wildness that frightened her. With Nick she was afraid she would go spinning out of control. And control was everything. Cyndi had placed her life in the hands of others on too many occasions. She had learned that didn't lead to happiness. She had become a careful person, wary of change, reconciled to a solitary existence.

But Nick made her want to be careless. Changed. One half of a pair.

How had he turned her upside down so fast? Surely that was symptomatic of a woman who didn't know what she wanted. Dear God, she had always thought she wanted romantic promises, but with Nick she didn't care if he promised her anything. He wasn't the smooth, urbane man of her dreams. He had ragged edges. Just being with him was demanding. And one touch of his hand could make her throb.

The water's caressing movements became unbearable as Cyndi again remembered Nick's touch. She dragged herself out of the tub and wrapped herself in a towel. As she shooed Lolita inside, cut off the garden lights and drew curtains, she tried not to think of the way Nick had palmed her breasts, the way his fingers had moved up her thighs, the way she had stood there trembling, reacting, aching for him.

In her bathroom, as she dropped the towel and reached for her robe, her reflection in the full-length mirror made her pause. Was that really her? she wondered. With her eyes somnolent, her face flushed, her breasts rosy tipped and heavy, she felt like a stranger in her own skin. She stepped closer to the mirror, her fingers tracing the outline of her reflected face. Who was this creature who looked so ripe, who trembled from the mere memory of a man's touch? This couldn't be the careful woman she thought she was. There was the ideal and then there was the reality. Where did they meet?

While she stared at her reflection, Cyndi realized all of her questions always led back to the central issue of who she was.

She had known the answer ten years ago. Everyone had their roles back then. Sonny had been the hero, Ryder the rebel. Jennifer was the eternal cheerleader, Meredith the calm, steady brain. As for herself . . . she really had been the princess, the one who always got what she wanted.

She wondered, if Sonny had lived, would they have gotten past those hurtful words he had flung at her in anger and frustration? Would he have remained a hero? And the rest of them—were they still the same? Or, like herself, had time and disappointment changed them, shaped them into individuals who had little in common with the teenagers she remembered?

Cyndi was tempted, as she had never been before, to call one of her old friends. They hadn't all been together since the prom. After the tragedy of Sonny's death, the entire senior class had been in disarray. They had been cruising toward graduation anyway, and no one had seemed to care that Cyndi didn't go back to school. For once, her mother had indulged her. Cyndi remembered long days spent lying in her bed, watching the pattern made on the ceiling by the May sunshine and the big oak trees in their front yard. Her father had brought her flowers and held her while she cried. At Sonny's funeral, as she had struggled with a load of secret guilt, her father had stood on one side, Devlin on the other, holding her up.

The next week she had roused herself enough to go to graduation, but Meredith, their class valedictorian, hadn't been there. Her parents said she had departed for a special study program before starting Vassar. Jennifer had talked to Cyndi, chattering in her frenzied, nonstop pattern about how busy, busy, busy she was going to be that summer. She hadn't mentioned Sonny. No one had said his name in front of her.

Cyndi had faced the summer, her whole future, with lethargy and disinterest until her mother decided enough was enough. She packed Cyndi off to Savannah to stay with her grandmother. Her Georgia cousins swept her into a social whirl, leaving her little time for moping.

In the fall, there was college. She met her future husband the first day on campus. Christmas break had been spent at his parents' home, where they announced their engagement. Cyndi, who couldn't bear to have the wedding in the Hazelhurst church where she had dreamed of marrying Sonny, had agreed to hold the ceremony in her groom's hometown.

If Cyndi ever thought of calling Meredith or Jennifer, she didn't remember the impulse. But now she was tempted. If she touched a part of her past, surely she could figure out her future, figure out the person she was supposed to have become.

"But that's crazy," she murmured, seizing her robe from the hook off the bathroom door.

But there was someone she could call for help. There was Lin.

If there was anyone who could help Cyndi sort out the jumble her life had become, it had to be Lin. Her brother could always be counted on for support, of course, but she wanted a woman's point of view. Lin had such a clear, unfettered way of looking at life. She would help Cyndi put everything—Nick included—in perspective. Reassured by that knowledge, Cyndi reached for the phone.

They met for brunch the next day, and at a palm-shaded table on the terrace of a popular restaurant, Lin listened to Cyndi's problems. Even with Lin it wasn't easy for Cyndi to talk about any of it, especially about Sonny and her mistakes with other men. But Lin, as always, was a good listener, sympathetic and attentive.

Lin said little until Cyndi started talking about her confusion over Nick. Simply, bluntly, she said, "I don't get it, Cyndi. Nick says he cares for you, and obviously, you have some pretty strong feelings for him. This is you and Nick, not you and Sonny, you and anyone else. Can't you just start from that premise?"

"I wish I could."

"Don't just wish. *Do.*"

Cyndi sat back in her cushioned seat. "It's not that simple, Lin. I thought I explained. Nick is too... too..."

"Dangerous? Too male? Too demanding?

Cyndi's fingers curled around the slender stem of her champagne flute. Nick was all of those things. "He's not right for me, Lin, or least he's not right for the person I thought I was." She sighed. "Whoever that woman is, of course."

"Lord, but you're confusing me," Lin muttered, pushing aside her half-eaten omelet. "Did Nick bring on this big identity crisis?"

Stung by what she perceived as derision, Cyndi retorted, "I'm not like you, Lin. I'm not sure of every move I should make."

"Is that how I am?" Dappled sunshine made silver bangles at Lin's wrist glint as she gestured toward herself. "That's certainly not how I feel ninety-eight percent of the time."

Mockingly Cyndi replied, "Oh, yes, and uncertainty is exactly how you became an executive producer at age twenty-seven. The young genius is so unsure. Yes, that's how you created this fabulous career."

"But you have a fabulous career, too," Lin countered.

"Which I owe entirely to other people."

"Do other people get in front of the camera with you every day?"

"Practically."

Lin made a soft sound of disgust. "You don't give yourself half the credit you deserve, Cyndi."

"So why do I feel like I'm going to fly into a million pieces at any moment."

"Because you're in love with Nick?"

"I don't know that I love him," Cyndi protested. "I'm not sure I can love anyone. That's the crux of the problem. I've always felt as if love was for other people. I never get it right."

"Maybe you haven't been in love with the right person."

"But how do you know who's right?"

Lin sighed and brushed a hand through her dark hair. "The age-old question. If I had the answer, I'd be selling it worldwide. We'd open up a television lovelorn ministry and make a fortune."

"Be serious."

"I am serious." Lin sat forward, her expression intense. "I can't tell you if Nick is the right person for you. Only you can find that out, and you won't make that discovery by sitting around talking to me about it or by mooning about past mistakes."

Cyndi flushed. Lin made her sound like a whining child.

Her friend continued in a softer voice, "The very first time I thought I was in love, I called Me—my mother—and asked her how I would know if it was the real thing." A smile touched Lin's features. "Me said love is like leaving on a long, unpredictable journey. She said you just have to start, to put one foot in front of the other and see where you go."

"So I should just start, right."

Lin nodded. "You're only at the beginning and you're anticipating your failure. It looks like a hard journey, but you won't know what happens unless you just start."

Cyndi knew, as Lin couldn't, how overwhelming Nick could be. Loving him would require strength and confidence. She was afraid both qualities were in short supply where she was concerned. "I may get lost," she murmured.

"But you'll survive." Lightly Lin touched the hand Cyndi still had wrapped around her glass. "You really are strong, Cyndi. You don't think so, but those of us who care about you know your strengths. And who knows? Maybe you and Nick will get it right."

"Oh, God," Cyndi breathed, filled with uncertainty. "I think I'm more frightened of falling in love with him than anything else. Because I know love won't solve all the problems."

"It's a frightening proposition, all right," Lin agreed. "Love doesn't come with a guarantee about happily ever afters."

Cyndi mused, "Do those endings really exist outside those stupid fairy tales they force-feed to little girls?"

"I'm not sure," Lin said. "But something worked for my parents. They endured separation and prejudice and unbelievable adjustments. I know without any doubts they would each walk through fire for the other. They love each other now." She dropped her gaze to the table. "And forever."

"A once-in-a-million kind of love."

"I want that, too," Lin said, her voice fierce.

Cyndi looked up in surprise. The thoroughly Americanized woman seated across from her in a smart navy-and-white sundress had never talked about wanting more than a fabulous career. Over dinners and lunches and the long hours she and Cyndi had spent working together during the past few years, the dreams she had shared were centered on her professional life. Marriage and children were nothing more than a far-distant possibility, locked away in a file marked "maybe." Lin dreamed of being *somebody*.

Like so many others who had escaped the country where she was born, she was filled with ambition.

But now there appeared to be something more in Lin's life. Her relationship with Jacob—whom Cyndi still hadn't met—was more serious than Cyndi had dreamed. "Are you in love with Jacob?" she asked.

Her friend's laughter was quick. "Wow, Cyndi, for someone who doesn't ask anything for weeks and weeks, you come up with pretty direct questions, don't you?"

Cyndi grinned. "Call this our honesty brunch. I've cried on your shoulder. Why shouldn't I return the favor?"

"Right." The laughter disappeared as Lin fiddled with the plastic umbrella that had decorated her fruit juice. "I love him," she said finally, glancing up at Cyndi. "I love him, and just like you feel about Nick, I have no idea if Jacob and I can have a fairy-tale ending."

"But if you're sure you're in love—"

"You said it all before. There are no guarantees."

"What's the problem?"

Bitterness crept into Lin's expression. "The same thing I've faced my entire life. I don't know if I fit in."

"That's crazy," Cyndi protested. "You fit anywhere, Lin. Anyone who doesn't think so isn't worthy of you."

"Oh, it isn't Jacob," Lin assured her. "I know he loves me. It's his family." She shifted in her seat, frowning. "He has three children—teenagers."

"So he's a little older than you? Is that what's causing the problems?"

Lin nodded. "The kids plus the entire family. Jacob comes from this tight-knit, Jewish family. His wife, who died about three years ago, was someone he grew up with. From what I can gather, she was this perfect wife and mother, the perfect hostess, the perfect everything. And now here I come—this much younger career woman who's Amerasian to boot."

"So you're different than she was. Surely that's not an insurmountable problem."

"You wouldn't think so." Lin took a deep breath. "But I met the clan last weekend, Cyndi. When I walked in, I felt the shock that went through the room."

Cyndi was distressed. "So Jacob hadn't prepared them for you?"

Lin laughed. "Jacob, romantic fool that he is, didn't anticipate problems. Even after last weekend, he still thinks there's nothing to worry about. He says we can make it, to give them some time to adjust to us. But I'm not so sure. We were talking marriage—"

"Lin!" Cyndi leaned forward, grabbing her friend's hand. "Marriage? You're talking marriage?"

"*Were* talking," Lin corrected. "I won't marry him if the family doesn't approve." She straightened her shoulders, her expression growing stony. "I won't go through that again, not being accepted. I can't forget how it was before Me and I came to America or the way my father's family treated us. I won't live like that, Cyndi."

"Surely Jacob doesn't want that, either."

"He's being unrealistic."

Cyndi paused then asked softly, "What happens if you can't resolve this?"

"Then I guess it'll be over."

Her hand tightening on her friend's, Cyndi felt her pain. "I hope that doesn't happen, Lin."

"Oh, God, Cyndi, I hope not, either." Lin blinked her eyes, as if fighting tears. "I love him so much. I never expected to fall in love like this. But it's true what they say. It feels as if Jacob is the missing part of me. He makes me whole."

Cyndi sat back, amazed by her friend's statement. Lin was the most complete-unto-herself person Cyndi had ever known. Yet it was a man who was making her feel whole. That wasn't the liberated view, the perspective she would have expected from someone as independent and confident as Lin. It was closer to what Cyndi had learned from her own mother about the importance of finding the right mate.

Cyndi had believed her mother was right for a long time. She had often identified herself by her relationships with men. She yearned to be someone's girlfriend, wife, lover. Only in the past year—when she had at last decided she could never fit those roles—had she begun to see herself as something quite apart from those men. She hadn't known exactly what her role was, but she had been searching for it.

And now there was Nick.

Perhaps the problem she'd had in the past was just as Lin had suggested—she hadn't belonged to the right men. Perhaps Nick, with his intensity and urgent demands, was the key that would unlock Cyndi's true self. Perhaps, just as Lin needed Jacob, she needed

Nick to make her complete. It was the same conclusion she had reached so often in the past, but maybe
with Nick it would be different. Like the dead end in
a maze, she kept coming back to that possibility as the
afternoon wore on.

When she and Lin left the restaurant, she met Jacob, who had come to take Lin to an afternoon mati-
nee. He was distinguished, graying and quite unlike
anyone Cyndi would have selected for her friend.
Cyndi stood on the sidewalk in the sunshine, watching the couple walk away, holding hands, laughing.
They could laugh, even though they had so much left
to resolve.

Envy sliced through Cyndi. She wanted a chance,
just a chance at love like that. Nick had resurrected her
hopes of love. She could feel them flowering. She
thought she was ready, as Lin's mother might say, to
start the journey.

"Punch it any harder, and you'll likely be buyin' me
a new one."

Sweet Pea's amused comment stopped the furious
assault Nick had launched at the punching bag. The
bag usually calmed him down. But not today. Honest
sweat wasn't going to purge Cyndi from his system.

Shaking his head, Sweet Pea drawled, "You look to
me like a man with a powerful lot on his mind."

Nick stripped off the gloves and tossed them onto a
nearby bench. "You always were an astute observer of
mankind."

"From that tone of yours, it sounds like woman
trouble."

Grunting, Nick pushed a towel across his perspiration-soaked hair.

"Don't tell you've done chased away that pretty lady you had in here last week?"

"Chasing wasn't necessary. It was her idea."

Sweat Pea whistled. "Lawsy-day, son. Why can't you hold on to a woman?"

Nick sat down on the bench and blew out a deep breath. "I obviously don't know what they want."

"Attention," the older man offered. "Lots of attention."

"For some women that's not enough."

"Then you must not be givin' her the right attention. Take her some flowers, take her dancin', get her outside and do some romancin'. Pretty soon I'll be gettin' my old tux out of mothballs for the weddin'."

Laughing, Nick shook his head. "You don't understand modern women, Sweet Pea. They make things a lot more complicated than that."

"That's a shame, when things could be so simple."

"Yeah," Nick mumbled. "Simple." There was no word in the English language that applied less to Cyndi Saint.

Sweet Pea offered him a hand up. "Go on, now, hit the showers. Get out of this gym. You might find out the pretty lady's changed her mind." Impudently, as he might have done when Nick was ten, he swatted him on the behind before ambling off to the other side of the gym.

Nick wished Sweet Pea was right about Cyndi changing her mind. As he had told her, he was willing to wait until she got everything sorted out. But would she sort it out? Would she even want to after the way he had left her in tears Thursday? He wasn't proud of that. Cyndi had been in a fragile, easily hurt state of mind. He should have exercised a little restraint.

He didn't pretend to understand all the forces at work inside her. But, dammit, he didn't want her hiding from the truth, either. Run and hide, run and hide—that was her pattern. Silently he cursed the young man, the *men,* who hadn't known how to appreciate her. Or how to love her.

Did he have the answers? Nick wasn't sure. But he believed the attraction that had pulled him and Cyndi together was worth exploring. Surely that attraction would bring her back to him.

He headed home from the gym and was irritated to find a car parked in his reserved space at his apartment building's parking garage. It took a moment for him to realize the car was Cyndi's. He sat, idling his Porsche's engine, staring at her small white BMW.

"Thinking of smashing it to bits?"

He turned to find Cyndi walking toward his car from the elevators. In her summer white dress, carrying a straw hat with a purple sash, she looked like a little girl dressed up for the Easter parade.

"The security guard let me come in and park," she offered. "He remembered me from last weekend. You know, I left my car here."

Nick didn't say anything, but sat, gripping the steering wheel as if it were all that kept him from floating out of the car. He was too afraid she was a figment of his imagination, conjured up because he had wanted her to come to him so badly.

"He's a terrible flirt," Cyndi continued.

Nick cleared his throat, finally trusting himself to speak. "He's just a sucker for a pretty face."

"That so?"

"Just like me."

Cyndi smiled then, a tentative smile, but the brim of her hat twisted in her hands, betraying her nerves. "When your car wasn't here, I went upstairs, thinking you might be home, anyway."

"I wasn't," he said unnecessarily.

She nodded, hesitated, then said, "Are you going to get out of the car, or what?"

"It depends on what you have to say to me." Nick loosened his death grip on the steering wheel. "If it's not something good, I think I'll just keep right on driving. I don't feel much like arguing or rehashing what we've already been over and over."

Ducking her head, she took a deep breath. "But I want to talk, Nick. I want to see if we can work this out."

He parked his car in a visitor's slot. He got out and approached Cyndi. He intended just to take her hand. What he didn't intend or expect was the way her arms slipped around him.

Head tipped back, blue eyes bright with emotion, she whispered, "Prove it to me, Nick. You said we could prove I'm capable of loving someone. I believe you." Her voice lowered, but her gaze held steady. "I want you."

"Oh, Cyndi," he whispered, cupping her face with his hands. "I don't think this is just about want. It isn't sex—"

"But that's part of it," Cyndi protested. "I'm not good at sharing myself, Nick. But I want to change that. I want you to change that."

It would have taken a stronger man than Nick to resist the sweetness Cyndi offered. Especially since he was a man in love. For years he had thought his heart was immune, but he hadn't counted on the woman he was holding in his arms.

"Come upstairs," he invited. "We'll talk."

The invitation was admirable. But once inside his apartment, they both seemed to forget about talking. The door barely closed behind them before Nick was kissing Cyndi. This time she put no barriers between them. She didn't resist or protest. She simply kissed him. Lips opening, tasting, tempting. She kissed him like a woman instead of a frightened girl.

Breaking away at last, she murmured, "I've been dreaming about your kisses."

"Only my kisses?" He allowed his lips to trail down her neck. His tongue traced the hollow at the base of her throat, and Cyndi dropped her hat to the floor. Her arms went around him again. Chuckling, he lifted his mouth back to hers. "You didn't answer me, Miss Saint. Is it only kisses you want?"

Her voice was breathless. "I don't think so."

His hands went to her hair, spreading the soft tendrils through his fingers. "Tell me," he whispered against her lips. "What else is in these dreams of yours?"

"Ecstasy," she replied, though a blush heated her cheeks. "Complete ecstasy."

He laughed. "You don't waste any time before putting pressure on a guy, do you?"

She pressed her face to his shoulder, sighing. "Just being held by you is heaven, Nick. Right now, you could just hold me, and I'd be happy."

He brushed a kiss to her hair and tightened his arms about her. "Then I'll just hold you, Cyndi. If that's all you want, that's what I'll do."

"No." She pulled away, her gaze searching his face. "I told you. That's not really enough. That's not what I want." Her lips settled on his once more. There was a demand in this kiss, an answer to his need where once he had tasted only questions.

Hunger leaped inside Nick as they kissed. Through the thin layers of material separating their bodies, he could feel Cyndi's breasts, soft and rounded, against his chest. He imagined them freed, the nipples pebbling in his palm, beneath his mouth. His body grew taut as his hands slipped to her hips and pulled her against him. He couldn't stop the groan of pleasure that built deep inside his throat.

Cyndi stepped back then. Her eyes were wide, darkened by desire and perhaps a bit of fear. But she took his hand and tugged him toward the stairs that led to his loft. "Come show me how to love, Nick."

He followed her up the steps.

His bed faced west, toward a wall of glass that framed a view of blue sky and the buildings that sloped downward toward the ocean. There was little in this expansive pine-planked room other than the bed and the square clean-lined table beside it. Broad, drenched by the afternoon sun, with sheets rumpled, the bed stood like an island, claiming all of Cyndi's attention as she paused at the head of the stairs. Nick started toward the windows, intending to close the blinds, but she stopped him, saying, "I want to be in the sun."

And moments later, when she knelt with him on the edge of the bed, he thought it appropriate that they faced each other in the light. He wanted no ghosts or shadows in this bed with them.

She was like quicksilver in his arms, restless, pliant. Her hands flowed over him so easily, too quickly. He tugged his T-shirt off, tossing it aside, eager for the feel of her fingers on his flesh. He closed his eyes as her hands glided across his shoulders and down his back. Her movements were slow, as if she were memorizing every inch of body. Her touch, such an innocent touch, sent him to the edge of excitement. He had to capture Cyndi's hands, hold them against his chest, while he fought for control.

"What's wrong?"

Her soft question made him open his eyes. "It's just too fast."

"I'm sorry." Flushing, she sat back on her heels, looking young and unsure. "I told you, Nick—"

He hadn't meant to cause her uncertainty. He pulled her to him again. "You didn't do anything wrong. There isn't a right or wrong here. Whatever you want—that's what's right."

"And if I don't know what I want?"

"We'll figure it out." Her hands spread across his chest, and Nick groaned, heated by her touch. "We'll work it out, baby, trust me, we'll make it work."

Then his mouth moved across hers, parting her lips, his tongue miming a more intimate coupling. With a cry that tugged at his heart, she clutched him closer. His lips roamed from her face to her throat till she arched her neck, allowing him to spread kisses downward. He lingered at the deep vee of her dress, where the buttons had parted to reveal a lacy slip. Breathing in her sweet, unmistakable scent, he fumbled with those buttons until she reached to help him. Soon the dress, then the slip, like gossamer wings in a shaft of sunlight, drifted to the floor.

Cyndi was trembling as Nick drew her down beside him on the tangled sheets. His desire for her had become one endless ache, but that didn't matter. What mattered was that he take the time to croon soft words against her skin. She was full of feelings she didn't know what to do with, that much was very clear. Nick wanted this to be right for her. He didn't think he had ever been a selfish lover, but this went beyond the giving of pleasure. Somehow, he had to reach deep within Cyndi, he had to find the very essence of her femininity, to prove how right this could be. Even if they didn't reach the ultimate, it could be right; she could share herself.

So he reined in his hunger. He stroked and soothed her. He was gentle, he was careful. He took it slow. What he wanted was to bury himself inside her, but they went one step at a time, making discoveries along the way.

He hadn't thought Cyndi's body would hold any surprises for him. He knew she was perfect. The tights and leotards she had worn so often had hugged and revealed every supple curve and firm muscle. But in wispy bra and panties she seemed much thinner, more fragile. Her skin was a pale honey. And when her bra was pushed aside, her breasts were paler still. Pale and firm. Irresistible. The coral nipples puckered, inviting his attentions. He obliged.

Cyndi went very still, her eyes drifting shut, as Nick stroked tiny circles around the hardening peaks of her breasts. Then his mouth was moving against her. Open, warm, indescribable—his mouth brought the wanting into a sharper focus. Time itself seemed to slow as he lathed one nipple, then the other, fueling her pleasure with unending patience.

He took such care with her. No one had ever tried so hard to please her. It made her want to please him. It created a connection between them that had as much to do with their heads and hearts as it did where he placed his hands or how he kissed her. Not that there was anything wrong with how he touched her, but there was a dimension to their loving that Cyndi had never experienced.

The touch of his hands was feather light, tracing low across her stomach, barely skimming the triangle of white lace and satin at the juncture of her thighs. Then his fingers pressed more insistently through the lace, and she grew moist. The need for him to touch her, *really* touch her, became insistent.

She had never felt quite like this before—with nerves stretched taut, with all the blood in her body seeming to flow downward toward one spot. She tried to tell him what she wanted, but the words came out as disjointed fragments that Nick shushed with another scorching kiss. He built the need inside her for what seemed like forever. When his fingers finally slipped beneath the lace and into the dewy, waiting cleft, she cried out, her hips rocking up off the bed.

She thought that was release. She was wrong. Release came as Nick stroked her. Somehow, he helped her to that place where she had never managed to go. The wild place. She had never dreamed it was so high. Or filled with hundreds of bright lights that exploded into hundreds more. They rained down in a shower of color and warmth. *She* rained down. Falling with the lights.

But Nick held her. With sighs and kisses and urgent touches, he pushed her back to that reckless, urgent place. He stripped away her panties, shoved his own clothes out of the way, melded their bodies into one seamless whole and joined her on another climb to the heights.

This time, they fell together.

Cyndi wasn't sure how long they lay in a sprawl of limbs, their breaths mingling, with hearts that thudded and finally changed to a steadier beat. When Nick withdrew from her, she turned on her side, still reeling from the onslaught to her senses. He pulled her back toward him, and they lay, spoon fashion, until the world settled into its rightful place.

These moments after lovemaking had usually been the most awkward for Cyndi. She had never known what to say or do. Often she had been embarrassed. Always, she had been left yearning for an elusive satisfaction. Today was different. She was sated. And Nick allowed no wall to go up between them. He kissed and cuddled, whispering to her about the way she had made him feel. The things he said, the way he said them, were graphic, erotic. They sent secret excitement curling through her stomach again. She was amazed.

Finally she turned round to face him and, with a smile, gently covered his mouth with her hand. "Do you always talk so much?"

He cupped her hand with is own, pressing a kiss against her fingers before drawing it away. "And haven't you ever heard of pillow talk?"

She replied, with mock seriousness, "Let's see, pillow talk, I think that was a Doris Day movie."

"Ha-ha." He rolled his eyes and laughed with her, but his expression grew serious as he stroked a hand through her hair. "How're you doing?" he murmured. "Okay?"

She felt the color stain her cheeks, a silly reaction considering all that had passed between them. She didn't, however, allow her gaze to drop from his. "Do you have to ask?"

He kissed her, a soft kiss, with lingering warmth.

Cyndi turned over on her back and stared at the ceiling, trying to remember each touch and sigh. It seemed incredible to her that she could lie here like this, naked and at ease with the man who had made her feel so much.

Nick propped himself up on bent elbow and gazed down at her. "What are you thinking?"

"I think you were right," she said without hesitation. "It really isn't about sex, is it?" When he didn't reply, she went on to explain, "I mean, what happened between us was sex, but it wasn't just physical. At least not for me. I mean, it was physical. You touched me, I touched you, but it was connected to something else.''

"It's all in your head," Nick replied, adding, "or your heart. The physical part's easy."

She cocked an eyebrow at him. "Oh, really?"

"Maybe I should say *easier*." He tapped her forehead gently with a finger. "The part up here's much more difficult, harder to control."

"But we controlled it today."

"Maybe it helped that I love you so damn much."

Startled, her gaze went up to his.

"No," he whispered before she could say anything. "Don't say a word. Don't tell me that I can't love you, or that you're no good at love, or that we don't really know each other. I've heard all those arguments, Cyndi, and I still love you."

Breathing his name, she moved into his waiting embrace. "I can't imagine why you love me. I know it's not easy—"

"That's not true. Whoever told you that was wrong. Loving you is one of the easiest things I've ever done."

She wanted to believe him. Like nothing else before, she wanted to believe in this man's love. They had started this journey together. She knew there would be more chance of success if he loved her. And especially if she loved him.

But Cyndi had exchanged words of love before. She had believed them before. She wasn't so trusting now. Even with Nick, who had just shown her a realm of sexual fulfillment she hadn't thought existed for her, she still didn't know if this was love. It was strange how she had come running to him, hoping for some quick answers. Yet still she had questions, about herself, about him, about what they might make together.

Perhaps Nick sensed Cyndi's uncertainty. For in his dark eyes there was a sadness, a puzzlement she had never seen. She longed to erase that look. At the same time, she didn't want to lie to him, to give him false assurances about what she felt. So she just touched him. Lovingly she traced the lines beside his mouth, her fingertips scraping against the stubble of his beard.

The freedom she felt to touch this man was in and of itself a wonder to her. Maybe, long ago, before sex had become an issue, she had known this sort of easiness with Sonny. She could remember ruffling his hair, touching his cheek, sharing kisses he hadn't wanted to be preludes to more. It was like that now with Nick, except the prelude was there, too. And it felt right, it felt so incredibly right.

Unself-consciously, she trailed a finger from his squared chin to his throat and allowed herself the luxury of appreciating his masculine body. Dark hair, mixed here and there with silver, spread from the center of his chest, down a narrow line to a flat belly, widening once more to a dark thatch above his sex. Her touch followed her gaze, and he stirred against her hand. As she looked back into his eyes, her touch grew bolder. She was pleased with her boldness. Nick was, too. He became heavy, hard with need.

And the whirlwind began again.

This time was unlike the first. There was no lingering, no pauses to savor each nuance of every movement. This was a fervent coupling, with her legs wrapped high around his hips, his hands hard against her buttocks as he found a rhythm that rocked them both to completion.

Exhausted, Cyndi fell asleep in Nick's arms. But he was gone when she awoke starving, sometime after the sun had set. The luminous digital readout on the bedside alarm clock said it wasn't quite ten o'clock. Cyndi could hear Nick's off-key singing coming from somewhere downstairs. She smiled into the darkness and switched on a light.

And there, beneath the lamp, beside the tumble-sheeted bed where she lay, was a vase of red roses.

Opened wide.

Shedding their blossoms.

Their perfume heavy in the air.

It was one of her most cherished images, one that seemed synonymous with love, brought to life. Cyndi touched one fragile bloom with her hand, wondering how Nick could have known about this romantic dream.

And she wished, fervently, that he would somehow know the way to make all her dreams come true.

Chapter Nine

I love Cyndi.

Like a kid reciting a favorite nursery rhyme, Nick repeated those words to himself often during the weeks after Cyndi became his lover. They drummed in his head while he sat waiting at a traffic light. When he glanced at an old photograph of his father. During a television commercial that extolled the romantic virtues of April and Paris and a shared cup of coffee.

He thought it might be nice to take Cyndi to Paris. They could view the Eiffel Tower, tramp through the Louvre and do every touristy, romantic thing he had never done with anyone else. He wanted to take her everywhere. To Boston to meet his sisters and their families. To a little restaurant he knew in Greenwich Village where, unashamed of clichés, the owners put checkered cloths on the tables, made candle holders from wine bottles and served spaghetti sauce that tasted just like his mother's.

Nick knew he was behaving like something of a fool. And he didn't care. He was carried away with loving Cyndi.

At the gym, Sweet Pea grinned and asked when he should break out his tuxedo.

And as an old friend who had seen Nick through one or two romantic entanglements, Harris Fielding was pretty smug about the whole situation, too. Over lunch one day, he joked, "Isn't there an old saying about how the mighty are fallen?"

"I don't know what you mean," Nick retorted.

Harris lounged back in his chair, grinning. "It's you—the original man-who-doesn't-need-anyone. Now you go around acting as if you've discovered the secret to happiness."

Nick thought of the sleepy smile Cyndi had greeted him with this morning. "Maybe I have."

"Uh-oh," Harris murmured. "I recognize that look. You look altar bound."

Though he laughed off the suggestion with Harris, the idea of marriage took root in Nick's mind. He let the fantasy play out even further, seeing himself and Cyndi with a couple of kids. Opening presents on Christmas morning. Playing catch in the backyard. Blowing candles out on birthday cakes. It wasn't a bad idea. Except for one problem.

Cyndi needed to love him, too.

He didn't like dwelling on that problem, because in so many respects he was utterly content. He and Cyndi were together almost every minute that they weren't working. Their lives seemed to fit like the precision parts of a high tech machine. The important people in her life—Lin and Devlin—liked him. Hell, even her cat had accepted his presence. Last weekend when he had stayed at Cyndi's house, Lolita had deigned to sleep snuggled up against his leg. It was only Cyndi who still held something of herself back from him. And he didn't know why.

Nick didn't understand half measures. As Harris had said, he had fallen and fallen hard. That meant he loved Cyndi completely, with nothing guarded. There wasn't any aspect of his life he didn't want to share with her. His work. His ideas and ideals. His body. And Cyndi shared . . . up to a point. Then she seemed to be watching, waiting for some misstep.

What did she expect him to do? That question weighed heavy on his mind one morning when he stopped by the studio. Last night, after he and Cyndi made love—spectacular, consuming love—he had felt her withdrawing from him. The barriers she put up to keep people out slid into place. He didn't know why the barriers were necessary with him, but she had gone home, seeming to prefer the solitude of an hour's drive to the comfort of sleeping in his arms.

He hadn't pressed the issue last night, but he wanted to clear up whatever was bothering her. They had made an agreement about keeping personal concerns away from the studio, so he was going to try to tempt her into an early lunch so they could talk.

She was taping an interview this morning. Nick watched her work, feeling proud. She was witty, bright, relaxed. And she knew it.

When the taping was over, she fairly pranced off the set, and in her dressing room, she threw her arms around him, crowing, "I was good, wasn't I? Pretty darn good!"

He grinned at her, enjoying her exuberance. When she was open like this, forgetting to measure every word, was when he loved her best. "You're beginning to like this job, aren't you?"

"Like?" Hugging her arms to her middle, she twirled around. "I love this job."

"And why is that?"

"Because I think I'm actually starting to be good at it. I'm still not perfect, but there are these moments, these fabulous moments, like today, when I can feel how right it is."

"You're getting cocky."

In answer, she kissed him. Hard. "Success is sexy, isn't it?"

"I don't know. Become successful and we'll see."

Her smile slowly faded.

Nick caught her hand. "Hey, you, I was kidding."

"No, no, you're right, I'm not a success yet."

"Cyndi—"

"We've all worked so hard that I keep forgetting there's a lot left to prove," she said, looking worried. "The show won't go on the air for another week and a half. We may bomb. I may bomb."

He kissed her nose. "I'll still love you."

Pushing away, she went to her desk. "It's not funny, Nick."

"Of course it's not funny, but I've told you before that you have to roll with the punches in this business."

"And I've told you before that I'm not like you." Almost angrily, she shuffled through some papers. "If this show fails, it means I've failed."

Her somber tone concerned Nick. Cyndi took everything to heart. He thought she'd carry the whole world on her shoulders if she thought it would fit. "You can't think of this as life or death," he advised. "It's just television, Cyndi."

She looked up. "*Just* television? This from a man who has dedicated his life to the tube?"

"Maybe I'm getting my priorities in order."

"I am, too," Cyndi retorted fiercely. "And I care about this show."

He spread his hands wide. "Fine. Good. You should care. I care, too. But if it doesn't work, I don't want to see you beating yourself up about it. You've fought the good fight, Cyndi. That's all you can do."

She turned away, mumbling, "You just don't understand."

"All right, explain to me how you feel."

Cyndi shook her head.

The irritation he had felt with her last night began inside him. "Dammit, Cyndi, you do these little shut-me-out routines, and it makes me so mad."

"I don't know what you're talking about—"

"Yes, you do," he insisted. "It's like last night. There was something wrong and you wouldn't discuss it."

Picking up an ink pen, she avoided his gaze. "I thought we had agreed to keep our personal lives out of the office."

"It's all related. You wouldn't confide in me last night. You won't talk to me now."

"Well, sometimes I might not want to talk. Especially when it's about things, feelings you'll never understand."

"You could try me."

She took a deep breath and threw down the pen as if in defeat. "All right, I'll explain. But since you've so rarely been unsure of yourself, I don't know how you can relate to the feelings I have about this show."

"Oh, for pity's sake, Cyndi, I've known some insecurity, too."

"For maybe five minutes, in between the jobs people are constantly offering you."

"Cyndi," Nick placated. "If this show doesn't work out, you'll still have a career. You've got the workout program, you've got an exercise video—"

"But I want this to be a success," Cyndi insisted. She did want to succeed. She wanted to make Nick proud. She didn't imagine he would ever understand how it felt to want to please someone as much as she wanted to please him. For Nick, life was one straight stride in the right direction. He was completely sure of where he was going, but if he happened to make a sidestep, he incorporated the deviation into his plan. He wanted to sweep Cyndi along with him, but there were times when he simply overwhelmed her.

Last night had been one of those occasions. He made such complete love to her; he stormed all her senses. He demanded her response. He gave her more than she thought possible but at the same time took what she hadn't known she had inside. On one hand, it was the fabulous, steamy sex she had never let herself hope to know. On the other, it was frightening because of how desperately she wanted to please Nick.

Pleasing Nick. Pleasing someone. It seemed she had spent her entire life pleasing everyone but herself.

Cyndi rubbed her forehead, trying to come up with the words that would explain how she felt. Before she could gather her thoughts, a knock sounded on the door, and without being invited, Lin stalked inside, her expression grim.

She tossed a folder onto Cyndi's desk. "We've got a problem. Take a look at the ads that are going to run for the show's premiere week."

Nick came around the desk while Cyndi opened the folder. From inside, her own image, clad in black leotard and flesh-colored tights, stared back at her. She was smiling in the photograph, with hands on her hips, her body turned in a flirtatious manner. Shocked, she dropped the folder to the desk and looked up at Lin. "This isn't the pose you guys chose, is it?"

"You've got that straight," Lin snapped. "I thought everyone agreed this kind of cheesecake wasn't the image we wanted you or the show projecting. I'd like to know who changed the concept."

Both women swung their gazes to a silent Nick.

"It isn't the way I thought it would be," he began.

"So you knew!" Lin sputtered. Cyndi was so startled she could only stare at him.

"The guys in the promotion department—"

Lin cut him off. "*Guys* is right! Maybe those bozos enjoyed this picture of Cyndi. I suppose most red-blooded American males would. But this show isn't for males. The target audience is women. And this ad is unacceptable. How could you let them do this, Nick?"

"I didn't *let* them," he returned, with an edge of impatience in his voice. "That department has some autonomy, Lin."

"This isn't autonomy. It's lunacy. This will alienate the very audience we want to attract. How in the hell could this have happened? We had concept meetings with the promotions people. Why did they ignore us?"

"They didn't ignore us," Nick said. "They just decided they wanted to do something a little different. They told me they were going with a leotard shot to capitalize on the audience Cyndi has from her other show."

Lin tapped the picture, her voice rising. "This isn't the way Cyndi presents herself on that show. I was there for this photo session. This wasn't even a serious shot. Cyndi was kidding around with the photographer, and we decided right after this that her outfit wasn't right. I don't know why the picture even got mixed in with the others. She looks like a tart, for God's sake."

Obviously losing the battle with his temper, Nick shot back at her, "You can stop screaming at me, Lin. I didn't know this was the photo they were going to use. I, of all people, don't want Cyndi looking like a tart to the whole country."

Finding her voice at last, Cyndi spoke up, "I want this changed."

When Lin and Nick continued to argue and ignore her, Cyndi raised her voice. "I said, I want it changed!"

The other two fell silent and turned to her in surprise.

Cyndi took a deep breath, willing her voice to remain calm. "Lin is right. This ad is unacceptable. Not only because of the show, but because of me, because of the way I feel. I won't be exploited this way."

"Nobody's trying to exploit you," Nick said quickly. "This was a mistake."

"A big one. And I want the ads changed."

Nick ran a hand through his hair. "That may be difficult. The show premieres in less than two weeks. The magazines have deadlines—"

"I don't care."

"Look, if they can't be changed, it's not the end of the world. I mean, you've spent several years in a leotard—"

"But not like this," Cyndi protested.

Lin interjected, "This gets the show off on the wrong foot, Nick. Can't you do something?"

"I'll try."

His unconcern annoyed Cyndi. "You don't think this is a problem, do you?"

After a slight hesitation, he replied, "Not like you two do, no."

Cyndi felt furious color creeping up her neck. She swallowed hard, not trusting herself to speak.

Lin had no such hesitation. Hands braced on her hips, she said, "I don't know why you're so cavalier about this. Where's Nick Calderaro, the perfectionist? You've put part of yourself into the development of this show, too. You agreed with *me* in those meetings with the promotion department."

Eyes narrowing, Nick nodded. "Yes, but in those same meetings, I said advertising this show in a couple of magazines is *not* what will build an audience. So I see no need in getting all upset about this and causing a big scene. When I was called about the change in photos for the ad, I let the promotions people do their jobs. They wanted something attention getting, something light and fun—"

"This isn't fun," Cyndi cut in, her words clipped and precise. "And I don't like it one little bit."

"I understand your feelings," Nick replied, his tone equally careful.

"Do you?" Lin asked. "Do you really?"

He lifted his hands in an impatient gesture. "Neither of you are listening to me. A group of ads won't make or break this show, and besides, there may not be a way to change them."

"There'd better be." Cyndi wasn't sure where the resolve in her voice originated, but fury was sweeping through her like a fever. She stood, hands clenching into fists at her sides. "When we sat in meetings, mapping out this show's format, we talked about making it intelligent, not some silly, giggling, throwaway hour."

Before Nick could protest, she began ticking items off on her fingers. "Professionalism, poise, control, preparation—those are what everyone has hammered into me for the last two months. These ads negate all of that."

With a firm but gentle touch, he took hold of her arms, his gaze steady on hers. "Cyndi, believe me. This isn't a big problem. Don't sweat the small stuff."

His patronizing tone infuriated her all the more, and she pulled away. "This isn't small to me. Maybe you have a dozen projects in the works for the network. But in case you didn't get the message before, let me repeat—this show is important to me."

"To me, too, dammit."

"Then change the ads."

"Cyndi—"

Snatching the folder off her desk, she started across the room. "All right, Nick, if you won't do something about this, I'll find someone who will. I'll go see Harris, or I'll go higher. If I remember correctly, I do have some friends in high places around here—"

Nick caught her elbow before she could reach the door, and there was no attempt to hide the irritation in his voice. "God, Cyndi, where is this prima donna act coming from?"

"Prima donna?" Anger made her tremble as she whirled to face him again. "Am I a prima donna because I'm fighting for something I believe in?"

"What you *believe* in?" The lines around Nick's mouth deepened into a stern pattern. "A few weeks ago, you seemed pretty content to let everyone else make decisions about this show."

"And that's the way you want me, right? You want the empty-headed blonde, the same one whose abilities you were so skeptical about in the beginning?"

"Of course not."

"Good. Because that's not who I am." It wasn't until the words tumbled out that Cyndi realized how much she meant them. For in her professional life, she was no longer the malleable person she had been only short weeks ago. Along with growing to love what she was doing, she had gained some measure, however small, of confidence. That was why she was fighting Nick so hard on this—because she believed she was right. For once, pleasing herself had become more important than pleasing someone else.

She took a deep breath. "These ads are going to be changed, Nick. You can do it, or I will. Take your pick."

They faced off for a few minutes, his gaze dark and furious, her chin lifted in defiance.

Finally, taking the folder she held out, Nick's reply was a sarcastic, "All right, *your highness,* you win this one." Then he was gone, the pictures on the wall rattling as he slammed the door.

From beside the desk, Lin murmured, "Damn, Cyndi, what got into you?"

Cyndi turned around slowly. She had been so angry she had forgotten Lin was even in the room.

"I mean, you were great," Lin continued. "But you're not usually that forceful."

"I wish I could have stayed calmer." Cyndi took another deep breath, trying to slow the thudding of her heart. "But when I saw that ad, I felt like a...a..."

"Piece of meat," her friend suggested.

Cyndi managed a slight smile. "Exactly. And I'm tired of just being this face and this body."

"You've never been just that, Cyndi. You know that."

"Do I?" Shaking her head, Cyndi returned to her desk. "I've spent most of my life being told my pretty face was what would bring me happiness and success."

"Not everyone told you that, surely."

"Just about." Cyndi sat, heaving a sigh. "Especially men. They think if you look a certain way, you're supposed to behave a certain way, too."

Lin perched on the edge of the desk and frowned at her. "Nick isn't only interested in what's outside. He's not that shallow."

"Oh, really? Remember, he thought I was just another blond bimbo."

"He doesn't now."

"No, right now, he thinks I'm a prima donna."

"He'll get over it. You'll prove him wrong." Lin smiled. "You and I are good at proving people wrong, aren't we?"

Cyndi wasn't sure of her own abilities in that respect. But she was sure of Lin. She fixed her friend with a steady regard. "If you believe what you just said, why is it you don't think you'll win over Jacob's family?"

Blinking, Lin sat up straighter. "Wait a minute, when did I become the subject of this conversation."

"We're talking about confidence," Cyndi retorted. "Something I've been lacking in, but which you've always had in abundance. Where's that confidence in respect to Jacob's family?''

Bowing her head, Lin was silent as she fiddled with the sleeve of her oversize teal jacket.

In a quiet voice, Cyndi continued, ''The person who told me she once took on an entire, hostile Nebraska farming community couldn't really have so much trouble with one little family, could she?''

Lin looked up, her eyes bright. ''There's a lot at stake with that family, Cyndi.''

''Wasn't there a family at stake in Nebraska, too? Your grandparents, cousins, aunts, uncles...''

''Not everyone accepted me.''

''For those who didn't, it's their loss. You can win over Jacob's family. I'm sure of it.''

Sighing, Lin said, ''I'd honestly rather take on the whole state of Nebraska.''

''Yes,'' Cyndi retorted, ''and it would be easier for me if I'd just walk away from that damn, complicated man who stormed out of here a few minutes ago.''

''You can't do that,'' Lin protested. ''That man means something to you. He's good for you, Cyndi. I know he is.''

''And isn't Jacob good for you?'' Cyndi paused until Lin nodded. ''Then you can't let him go without a fight.''

Her expression growing thoughtful, Lin stared at a point above Cyndi's shoulder. Finally she said, ''You're right. Of course you're right.''

"It shouldn't really be such a tough fight," Cyndi said. "Jacob believes in you, loves you. He's on your side."

Now it was Lin's turn to switch the subject. "Isn't that exactly the way Nick feels about you?"

Cyndi sat back, drumming her fingers on the arms of her chair. "Maybe," she said carefully.

"Then what is the problem? If there is one," Lin added hastily. "When you're not fighting over magazine ads, you two seem pretty tight these days."

Cyndi had to agree. Except for those times when her worries took over, the past few weeks with Nick had been wonderful. But that was what she didn't trust—the wonderfulness of it all. "Maybe we're too tight," she said. "Too good to be true. That's probably why I keep expecting to screw up, to disappoint him."

"Disappoint him? How?"

"A thousand different ways."

Lin shook a finger at Cyndi. "There you go again, not giving yourself enough credit. You've got to stop that." Turning, she headed for the door. "Stop expecting the worst to happen." With that hardly original advice she left Cyndi alone.

And it was good advice, but not so easy to put into action. Cyndi had a lifetime of dashed expectations with which to contend, and she hadn't Lin's buoyance or sense of self to guide her. She wondered if Lin had been born with those qualities, or if not, how her parents had managed to endow her with the resilience and hope she needed to make it through the twists and turns of life? And what was it Cyndi's own parents had done wrong?

Cyndi leaned back in her chair, wondering if her mother's critical, rather pessimistic nature could be blamed for her own insecure mind-set. Partially, perhaps. But she couldn't blame Fran Saint for Sonny's death or for the bad choices Cyndi had made since. If only she could put aside those failures and move forward with Nick. But no matter how she tried, she couldn't think of the future without the past pulling her backward.

It was all such a struggle. A struggle to believe Nick really loved her. A struggle to sort out her feelings for him. Was love supposed to be such a struggle? There had been a time when she imagined love as an effortless glide, one step flowing into the other, all leading to a happily ever after.

"A princess's life," Cyndi murmured, smiling slightly. She wouldn't have that with Nick. Nothing would ever be effortless with Nick. Even if they loved each other, he was too volatile, too demanding to make life anything but a challenge.

So how could she love him?

There was a sensible, adult part of Cyndi's brain that told her what she felt with Nick might very well be plain, ordinary lust. He had awakened her sexuality, helped her discover a buried part of her self. But Nick wanted more than sex. He had made that clear from the beginning. Cyndi wasn't sure she could give him what he wanted.

"But I have to love him," she whispered to her empty dressing room. Only a fool wouldn't love a man like Nick. For all of his demands, he was also fun-loving. He could raid the refrigerator with her at two in the morning. He and Devlin would compete over video games like two small boys. He liked drives up the Coast and watching movies in bed. Each day with Nick was like opening an unexpected gift. One time you might get sunshine and smiles. The next he would be brooding and intense. He was never predictable.

True to form, he showed up on her doorstep that very evening, proferring a dozen red roses and an apology. It wasn't that she thought their disagreement over the show's advertising would become a big issue, but she also hadn't expected him to admit a mistake.

"I was wrong," he said after she had asked him inside. "That ad is important to the show. And it's important to you. I shouldn't have argued about it."

"It's okay," Cyndi said, ready to forget the entire incident. She still wasn't sure where she had found the chutzpah to stand up to him.

"No, it's not okay. And I've taken care of it. The ad will be changed." Standing in the center of her living room, Nick shifted from foot to foot, looking uncertain, an unusual state for him. "I'm especially sorry for the prima donna crack. That's not you, Cyndi. That's never been you. That's one thing that makes you so different."

"For a minute I wasn't so different, though, was I?" At his frown, she continued, "I'm sure the way I acted reminded you of Nancy—the woman in New York you told me about."

"Well, maybe," he admitted, the barest trace of a grin curving his mouth. "But Nancy would've been throwing things against the walls."

"I'll keep that in mind," Cyndi murmured. "Sounds like a good strategy for next time."

His smile made another fleeting appearance. "That's not your style. But you did make me realize a few things today."

"That I have some opinions worth listening to?"

"I always knew you had opinions. It was just rare for you to express them the way you did today. A month or so ago, you would have let Lin do all the talking."

She felt rather pleased with herself. "Maybe I'm ready to fight my own battles."

Nick nodded. "It goes back to what you said this morning. You love what you're doing. You're beginning to trust your own talent."

"Talent? I don't—"

"Don't say you're not talented."

Smiling at his fervent tone, she quoted something he had once said to her. "You mean I'm not just a plastic form and a pretty smile?"

He looked more uncomfortable than ever. "I actually said that, didn't I?"

"And at one time it was probably true."

"No, you've always had something special. Lin told me once that it was your eagerness to please. I think it's your innate poise."

"Poise? Half the time the camera's on me, I feel ready to fall apart."

"It rarely shows."

"It's my mother's training," Cyndi said. "A lady never shows her emotions. She's always calm and collected."

Nick stepped closer, his expression changing. "That works fine in front of the camera. Not so fine elsewhere. You shouldn't always hide real emotions."

Because she didn't want to deal with what she knew he was leading to, Cyndi took the box of roses he still carried and dipped her head to catch their flower-shop fragrance. "Mmm, you can always apologize like this. I do love roses."

"They're not for the disagreement we had this morning. That was business." He cleared his throat. "The flowers are for last night. For whatever it was that I did that made you want to leave."

She looked up, touched by his gentle tone. "Nick, you didn't do anything."

"Then why'd you run away and leave me alone?"

"I wasn't running away." She sighed and started toward the kitchen. "Let me go put these flowers in water...."

"There you go again," Nick accused, "running away."

She paused. "I'm going to find a vase—"

"And when you come back, you'll find another way to avoid this conversation."

He wasn't going to let her get away this time. Cyndi set the box of roses on an end table and faced him, her arms folding defensively across her middle. "All right, Nick, what are the important issues?"

"How much I love you."

The intensity in his voice and his gaze made Cyndi take a step backward.

"No running," Nick said firmly. He took her by the hand and led her to the couch. The soft cushions gave under his weight as he sat beside her and loosened his necktie.

She started to get up. "Nick, you're tired. You should sit back and let me get you a beer—"

"Don't move," he ordered, pulling her to his side again. His arm slipped around her. "Indulge me, okay? Just sit here for a while and let me hold you." She stopped protesting and snuggled closer, her head resting on his shoulder.

He laid his cheek against her soft hair. "I've wanted to do this all day, you know. Ever since you left me last night—"

"I didn't *leave* you," Cyndi protested again. "I just came home. I wanted some time to myself. It's nothing for you to be all bent out of shape about."

"I guess I'm selfish, or something, because I want you with me all the time, every night. I love you." When she stiffened, he added, "My saying that makes you uncomfortable, doesn't it?"

"No, of course not."

"You're a rotten liar, Cyndi."

She pulled away and turned sideways on the couch, facing him, her blue eyes darkening with worry. "I feel as if I'm caught up in this stampede with you. We keep charging forward. It's all so fast."

"I'm not a kid," Nick whispered. "I don't see any reason to be waiting when I know what I want."

"And what is that?"

He cupped her face with his hands, wanting to tell her his daydreams about weddings and babies, daydreams he had never had until her. But instead, he simply said, "You, Cyndi. That's all I want."

She covered his hands with her own. "And you've got me."

"Not all of you," he whispered.

She didn't deny it. She simply sat there, looking miserable. Sighing, Nick let his arms fall to his sides and eased back against the cushions. He thought, with a brief stab of jealousy, of the boy Cyndi had once loved. *Sonny.* Such a silly name, one the boy surely would have grown to hate if tragedy hadn't taken his life at such a young age. Cyndi had loved Sonny before time and disappointment had taught her to guard her heart. Or had Cyndi been so in control of herself, even then? Had Sonny struggled to be sure of her? If so, Nick felt some sympathy for the boy.

He felt like something of a boy himself, full of impatience and youthful passion. Yet it wasn't all flash and fire, either. For the first time in his life, he understood the tie that had held his parents together. They had been bound by something deeper than passion. Nick had searched for that elusive connection with other women. Only Cyndi had given him a clue as to what it was all about.

"You do something to me," he said, looking at her. "You make me need you. Before you came into my life, I was so sure I didn't need anyone."

"I need you, too," she said.

"Do you? Do you really?"

She leaned forward, brushing her lips across his. "You can't doubt that I need you. You know the way you make me feel. You know no one else has ever made me feel like that."

Nick had been talking about emotional not sexual needs. But sex was the one area where he had no doubts about Cyndi. When she was in his arms, when she trembled beneath the touch of his hands, he didn't have to wonder about her feelings.

Wanting to erase his doubts, he pulled her closer. "I want to fill you," he murmured against her mouth. "I want to fill you so full of love that you'll love me back. Say you love me, Cyndi, please." But instead of waiting for her reply, he kissed her.

Nick made the kiss a demand. Hard. Deep. He kissed her until she sprawled across him. The wildness came, the way it always did when he kissed her. Just knowing he could coax that sort of response from Cyndi fueled Nick's own need. They kissed until she was in his lap, her hips straining against his own. She suggested they go to her bedroom, but Nick ignored her. He wanted her now. He needed to possess her, to know they were as one, if only in the most physical sense.

Impatiently he dispensed with her loose white T-shirt. Braless, her breasts were firm, the nipples peaked, ready for his attention. As his tongue circled each puckering, tantalizing bit of flesh, he grew harder. Cyndi's hands were in his hair, holding him tight against her. Her sweet scent surrounded him. Her sighs of pleasure filled his head.

With frenzied movements, they struggled to push clothing off or at least out of the way. Then Cyndi lowered her body to his, taking him deep inside. She was warm, moist, incredibly welcoming. Then she began to move, with Nick arching to meet each of her downward thrusts.

And they soared.

Locked together, murmuring unintelligible words of satisfaction, they clung to the highest point before beginning the descent.

But Nick wasn't ready to let Cyndi go. While her body still trembled from the onslaught, he laid her back on the couch and filled her again. It was as if he had lost all reason. He forgot about the birth control they had been using since their first, foolishly unprotected lovemaking. He let go of everything except the feel of her smooth skin, the salty taste of the moisture that beaded between her breasts, the searing release as he emptied his passion into her.

Yet even in those moments of heart-thudding, breathless climax, Cyndi didn't say she loved him. Those three words would have cost her little at that moment but still she held them back.

Nick tried to set aside his disappointment.

What did she need? he wondered that night and the next and the weeks that followed. He kept thinking of the night Cyndi had told him about Sonny's death. He remembered she'd said that with every man she'd known, she'd given and given of herself and received nothing in return. He didn't want that to be true of him. But he also didn't know what else to offer her. She had his love. Why wasn't that enough?

He couldn't reach the hidden part of her. She wouldn't let him reach it. He did his best not to resent her for that.

Cyndi could feel Nick's growing frustration. He wanted a commitment from her, something other than the sharing of bodies and beds. The more he said he loved her, the more she felt she had to lose and the more frightened she was. In her experience, love didn't last, and when she allowed herself to need someone too much, that's when they turned on her.

Nick said she was the woman he had been searching for his entire life. That was a big responsibility, and as always Cyndi took it to heart. She wanted to be the person he needed her to be; she didn't want to let him down. She felt as if he had placed her on some pedestal. And she knew she was going to fall. She always fell; she always shattered the illusions men had about her.

It was only a matter of time before Nick would realize she wasn't his golden girl.

Chapter Ten

"You're just going to love this."

Nick glanced up from his desk, surprised by the way Harris had barreled unannounced into his office. His friend was agitated, his normally sad eyes blazing as he waved the morning newspaper in the air and ranted about a review.

"Have a seat," Nick said. "Take a deep breath, calm yourself."

Harris tossed the newspaper onto the desk in front of Nick. "Read this. Then tell me to calm down."

Quickly Nick scanned the television review column. Then he bolted out of his chair and the office. Harris called after him, but he didn't pause. He needed to get to Cyndi.

After checking the show's production schedule, Nick drove to a pier where Cyndi was taping a fashion show segment with a popular beachwear designer. She was busy and there wasn't time for them to talk, but one look at her face was all Nick needed to know she had already read the review of her show. Because she had become a professional, because she had that innate poise, she carried on as if nothing were wrong. But Nick knew her well enough to see the tension that simmered just below the surface. It was in her too-bright smile, in the nervous movements of her hands, in the way she kept glancing at him.

She was devastated.

Thinking it best not to distract her with his presence, he retreated to the perimeter of the set. Lin, who looked glum, came to his side and handed him a cup of coffee. "I suppose you've read the morning paper."

"Don't let it bother you, Lin. The guy obviously doesn't understand what we're trying to do here."

"Oh, I can handle criticism. It's her I'm worried about." Lin nodded toward Cyndi. "She heard one of the crew discussing the review after she got here this morning, so of course she had to read it right away."

"And she was really upset, right?"

Lin shrugged. "You know Cyndi. She just got all tight-lipped and quiet. But the reviewer had some pretty harsh words about her in particular, so you can imagine how she took it."

"That's why I drove out here. She's got to understand that a review is one person's opinion."

"And lots of people like what we're doing. After less than three weeks on the air, we're already getting some positive mail about the show."

Nick swallowed a bitter, lukewarm sip of coffee and nodded. "The final judgment rests with the viewers. How many shows all over the television dial have the critics panned?"

"Plenty," Lin agreed, although her usual smile was noticeably absent. "I just wish this reviewer weren't read by millions of people."

"We could look at it as publicity." At Lin's venomous look, he explained, "Hey, at least they listed the right title, the right times and the right network."

"Oh, yeah, we should be happy about that, shouldn't we?"

Nick patted her on the shoulder. "Cheer up. We'll probably become a ratings killer, and critics everywhere will spend lots of time musing over our mysterious popularity."

Lin didn't look as if she believed him, but she was soon summoned elsewhere by an assistant sporting a mobile phone unit. Cyndi and her guests were still hard at work. So Nick took off his jacket and stood in the sun to watch the proceedings.

He dreaded discussing this review with Cyndi. Surely she understood a slam or two just came with the territory. Nick had never paid too much attention to reviews. He respected the opinions of colleagues, but the observations of those who set themselves up as experts without actually having worked in the medium mattered little to him. Cyndi wouldn't see it that way, he knew. As was true in every facet of her life, she wanted, *needed* to be perfect.

The review said she wasn't.

The taping seemed to drag on forever, but when it was over Nick hustled Cyndi into his Porsche. They drove aimlessly, dodging traffic down side streets, at last taking the freeway. Nick wove in and out of lanes. He didn't say a word. Neither did Cyndi. She just sat, with the wind blowing her hair into a golden cloud around her face, until he took an exit and pulled into his favorite taco stand. He bought lunch, which they ate in the car in relative silence.

"Are you going to talk about it?" he finally asked.

She heaved a long, miserable sigh. "I guess you're disappointed in the review."

"Not really. I think that the show is exactly what we set out to create and that it works very well. I don't need the opinion of some faceless guy to give me satisfaction."

"Lucky you," Cyndi said bitterly.

Nick lifted her chin with his fist. "Talk to me. I'm not going to let you curl up into a miserable little ball over there."

"You don't think he made some valid points?"

"Valid points? Let's see." Tossing taco wrappers to the floorboard, Nick fished the paper from where he had stashed it in the inside pocket of his jacket.

"Don't read it again," Cyndi implored, aghast.

"No, now, let's study it objectively." He spread the paper out on the steering wheel. "On the plus side this guy writes, '*A Better You*'s concept is hardly original, but the fast-moving format and slick graphics give it a stylized, sophisticated tone.'" Nick glanced up. "So far so good, isn't it?"

"Yes, and it was you who made the final decision on format, and we already know Lin and Joe are brilliant. Read what he says about me."

"Okay." Nick turned back to the newsprint. "He starts out by saying, 'The show's host, Cyndi Saint, is bright and attractive.' I don't see anything wrong with that."

Cyndi snatched the paper away. "He also said I appeared stiff in many segments." She scanned through the column, finding the most offensive phrases. "Right here, he says, 'Though Miss Saint has already proven to be perky and enthusiastic on her popular aerobic workout program and videotapes, her interview skills are still developing. With cable expansion slowing and the competition tightening, one has to wonder why the Choice Channel Cable Network selected a relative novice to host a show for which they have such high hopes. Perhaps they see something in Miss Saint beyond her spectacular good looks. This reviewer doesn't."

"He's wrong," Nick said with firmness. "Dead wrong."

She studied the review in silence for a moment more. "But he's saying exactly what you thought when I was offered this job."

"Cyndi—"

"Don't bother denying it."

"All right," he admitted, "so I didn't expect you to do well."

"And obviously, I haven't."

"Or so this guy thinks. And who is he? Some dimwit who flunked out of film school, probably."

Crumpling the paper into a ball, Cyndi gave a sarcastic laugh. "Oh, yes, he's so dim, he's one of the most respected reviewers in the country. He's written books about television and its impact on daily life. So, of course, I should just discount his opinion right away, shouldn't I?''

''That's right,'' Nick shot back at her. ''You should forget it. Pick yourself up, dust yourself off and forget it. Rule number one is that you never please everyone.''

''But it helps to please the important people.''

''Hey, I'm important and I'm pleased.''

There was a skeptical look in her eyes before she turned away. ''You don't write a column that's syndicated all across the country.''

''No, honey,'' he drawled, ''but I do decide which shows and people stay and which ones go from this network's daytime lineup.''

She looked at him again, her blue eyes widening. ''You wouldn't keep me on just because we're involved, would you?''

The question startled Nick. ''How could you even consider that?''

''I don't want special treatment.''

''Have I treated you special? Seems to me I've been pretty darn hard on you. At least that's what you and Lin said in the beginning.''

''In the beginning, yes—''

''And I haven't changed,'' Nick cut in. ''I still expect you to be the best, Cyndi. Whatever happens between us at the studio has nothing to do with the fact that we're personally involved.''

''But everyone else probably wonders, don't they? I mean, imagine what this reviewer would have said if he got hold of any personal information about us.''

''He'd probably think you slept your way to the top.''

"Nick!"

He caught her hands. "Cyndi, I'm kidding. We haven't given anyone reason to believe our relationship affects your job. And even if someone does think it, what does it matter? Everyone else's opinions aren't important."

"Maybe not to you. But I don't want anyone thinking I slept with you to keep my job."

Impatient with her dogged pursuit of the matter, he started the car and slammed it into gear. "You're inventing problems," he muttered as he executed a neat U-turn onto the highway. "You've let a bad critique of the show get you rattled. You need to just forget it."

Cyndi tried. She was intelligent enough to realize on her own what Nick had told her—one bad review wasn't the end of the world. She only wished the review hadn't so closely paralleled Nick's initial opinion of her. He said his opinion had been changed, that her hard work and growth impressed him. But an ugly thought had been planted in Cyndi's head. She wondered if he was really impressed with her or if he told her that because he loved her. Maybe, secretly, Nick wished he had pushed harder to keep her off the show.

The question nagged at her during the next few weeks. Every time she was in front of the camera she thought of those negative remarks. Was she being stiff? Was she prepared for the interview? Was her makeup too heavy, her clothes too flashy? If Nick was in the studio or on location, she searched him out for a critique. She asked for memos about each show after it aired. He thought that was silly, but she insisted. She didn't breathe easy until he gave her his approval.

In an attempt to strengthen her interviews, she doubled her preparation time, staying late at the studio or bringing background notes home with her to study. Normally most of her questions were prepared by Lin or one of the writers or assistant producers. But Cyndi thought her stiffness might lessen if she had some input to those questions.

Her increasingly frantic schedule led to some difficulties with Nick. He wanted more and more of her time and attention. Cyndi felt as if she were being pushed to the limit of her resources. She struggled to be at her peak on the job and in her private time with Nick.

At the end of several weeks she found herself putting Nick off when he suggested dinner or a movie or even a night at home. For several days running, she went home alone to get some work done. Finally he insisted on a quiet dinner out and followed Cyndi to her place. Yet still she stole some moments to work.

"You're becoming even more obsessive than you were," he told her as she sat at her desk, surrounded by research material.

Blinking, Cyndi glanced up, prepared to protest. But the words died in her throat. Nick stood in the open doorway to the walled garden off her bedroom. He had just showered, and an incongruous pink towel rode low on his lean, very masculine hips. Lolita was twining herself around his bare legs. Cyndi didn't really blame the cat. He looked like someone any female would love to curl up with.

Leaning against the opened door, Nick's smile was sexy, teasing. "It's an awfully nice night. Why don't you put away that mess and come out to the hot tub with me?''

A light breeze swept in the door, carrying the scents of earth and the potted flowers that lined the garden. Cyndi was tempted, oh so tempted to join Nick. But tomorrow's guest was a change of pace for her, a rather serious interview with a celebrity who had won a battle with cancer. It would be one of Cyndi's most challenging segments yet. So she shook her head at Nick's offer. "I have to be prepared for tomorrow."

He strolled over to the desk. "You couldn't be any more prepared." Ignoring Cyndi's protests, he closed her folders one by one. "What you need to make tomorrow a success is a fabulous night."

After the week of late nights Cyndi had put in, sleep qualified as fabulous in her mind. But she didn't think sleep was what Nick intended as he took her hand and pulled her from her chair and outside to the garden.

"Let's see," he murmured once they stood beside the tub. "How can we make sure you have a totally relaxing experience, Miss Saint?"

"You sound like a leader at a spa."

He grinned. "Think of this as your own personal spa." His smile deepened. "A pleasure spa. Now, first, you've got on too many clothes." Pausing every moment or so for light, sweet kisses, he dispensed with her cotton nightshirt and panties. His towel dropped, too. "Next, you need to be properly kissed." His lips moved slowly against her mouth, opening so his tongue could tease hers. Then he drew away. "And finally, we slip into the tub."

The minute the warm bubbling water closed around her, Cyndi knew Nick had the right idea. This was what she needed to relax. But relaxation wasn't the only thing on Nick's mind. He reached for her immediately, his hands moving from her breasts to her thighs. His kisses were gentle butterfly flutters along her throat and shoulders. She arched her neck, trying to put everything but Nick's touch out of her head. Normally it was so easy to let the world slip away and allow him to take over. And his touch *was* pleasant. But other thoughts kept intruding. Should she invest money in a voice coach? What should she wear tomorrow? Where would Lin . . .

"Hey, Earth to Cyndi, come in, Cyndi."

Looking up, she realized Nick had stopped kissing her. "I'm sorry," she murmured, lifting a hand to his beard-roughened cheek. "I was thinking."

He smiled. "Don't think. It's bad for you at moments like this."

"This?"

"Yes, this." Cupping her cheek, he kissed her again. Deeply. His hands slipped from her face to her breasts. With ever-narrowing circles his thumbs traced the hardening peaks. Nibbling at her earlobe, he whispered, "Are you thinking now?"

Cyndi shook her head and willed her body to relax. What was wrong with her? Usually Nick's attention was enough to reduce her to a quivering, yearning mass of need. But tonight she couldn't conjure up one ounce of interest. She was just so tired. So distracted. If only she didn't have that big interview.

"I'm beginning to get a complex," Nick said, drawing away. "You're not into this at all, are you?"

She had never refused him, never wanted to refuse him. The hot pleasure she found in his arms was the one sure thing about their relationship. Besides, men didn't like women who said no. So Cyndi shook her head and once more tugged Nick into her arms. "Of course I'm into it. I'm always willing and ready for you."

That didn't bring the expected response. Frowning, Nick pulled her arms from around his shoulders. "This isn't for me. It's for us."

"That's what I meant." She slipped forward, touching her mouth to his chin.

But again he held her away. "If this isn't what you want, Cyndi, I don't want it, either."

"But I told you. I *do* want you."

"I don't think so. And it's okay. Really it is." Moving to the other side of the tub, he leaned back in the water, closing his eyes.

Cyndi followed him. "Nick, please. I want to make love with you. I always want to make love."

"No, you don't."

She was frozen, immobilized by his simple statement. The one sure thing in their relationship was being questioned. Alarmed, she swallowed hard. "Nick, are you trying to tell me something?"

He opened his eyes. "Like what."

"Like I don't satisfy you."

For a moment he just stared at her. Then his mouth hardened into a thin line. "How can you ask that?"

"You said I don't always want to make love."

"Nobody always wants to make love."

"But I *always* want you."

"You didn't tonight."

She moved toward him. "Yes, I did. I'll show you."

His frown deepened. "Cyndi, you don't have to show me anything. So you didn't want to make love." He shrugged. "There'll be other nights."

"But you're angry."

"Yes, I'm angry, but not because you weren't in the mood. That's just life. It's not something to make a federal case out of. I'm angry because you seem to think I'd want you to do something you're not willing to do."

"But part of being with someone, of having a relationship, is being able to set aside your reluctance, to put your partner's needs before your own."

"Your partner's needs?" Now his eyes widened. "Damn, Cyndi, you sound like you're quoting from a pop psychology sex manual."

"But it's the truth, isn't it?"

"I bet your mother told you to close your eyes and bear it? Did you believe that, too?"

"Nick!"

"Well, you sound just about that archaic."

"But wouldn't you set aside your feelings to please me?" she retorted. "And don't say no, because I know you have. I've felt you holding back."

"Holding back is just part of making love. It makes it better for me, for both of us. And just because I've never been reluctant to make love with you doesn't mean it won't happen. A person gets tired or edgy—"

"A person can ignore those feelings, too." Once again, she put her arms around him. "I can be there for you, Nick. Anytime you want me, I can be there."

"Thank you," he said grimly. "Thank you so much for volunteering to be a willing receptacle for the spilling of my passions."

His sarcasm hurt. "Nick, that's not what I meant."

"Good, because if you think that's all that's involved when I make love to you, you're sadly mistaken. I can take care of sheer physical release all by myself, thank you."

"You're deliberately misunderstanding me."

"No, I'm not." Moving away from her, he swung out of the tub. In the light from the lanterns recessed in the wall, the water glistened on the hard muscles of his body. He looked completely, magnificently male. And he was furious.

Snapping his towel up, he said, "I don't know which of the men in your past planted this particular warped idea in your brain, but you can forget it. I'm not interested in having someone willingly sacrifice herself for my needs." He spun away but then turned back to her, hand outstretched. "Is that how you think of the way we make love, Cyndi? Is it just willingness?"

She straightened, the night air cool on her shoulders while the warm water bubbled around her breasts. "Of course it's more than that."

He stepped toward the tub. "But a minute ago you were asking me if you satisfy me. I don't know why you would need to ask. Can't you tell?"

She couldn't keep her mind from turning to the other men she'd known. Unlike the frank sexual talks she had with Nick, she hadn't known what was going on in those men's heads. She tried to explain. "In the past—"

"The past?" He swore, an eloquent profanity that told her just what he'd do with her past if he could. Obviously struggling with his temper, he turned away, flinging a towel around his neck, securing another at his waist. Cyndi climbed out of the tub and slipped on her nightshirt. It clung to her body in damp patches but alleviated her vulnerability.

Nick turned to face her again, his voice under tight control. "I'm tired of hearing about the past, Cyndi. When are you going to realize where you are, who you're with? I'm not those other men."

"I know that."

"Do you also know that I love you?" His outstretched hand closed into a fist. "I mean, I know you hear me tell you. I tell you all the time. I try to show you with everything I do. But I don't think you believe me."

She took a deep breath, and she didn't bother denying his accusation. "It isn't easy to believe you, Nick."

Hurt replaced the anger in his face. "But why?"

"Maybe it seems impossible that anyone could love me the way you say you do."

He dragged a hand through his hair and swore again. "You know what? I'm beginning to feel a little schizophrenic about this relationship we're supposed to be having. It's as if I'm having one relationship, while you're having another."

"That's not true."

"But you're missing part of the connection. Remember the first time we made love? You said afterwards that you finally understood how your head and your heart were as much a part of sex as your body. That's how it has to be in the entire relationship, Cyndi. That's how it is for me. I am completely, irreversibly in love with you. And I want you to open your eyes, open your heart to me. Let me in."

"I'm trying, Nick."

"What is it you're so unsure of?"

"Myself," she retorted, without considering her words. The confession just tumbled out. "It's me I don't trust. I don't trust myself to be the person you need."

"But you are the person I need."

"And when you change your mind?"

With a sigh of impatience, Nick threw back his head and stared at the night sky. Why did she continue to doubt herself, to doubt his feelings for her? "Cyndi, I know you've been hurt—"

"And I hurt other people, too."

"You mean Sonny?"

"He's only the most important, because I sent him away to die."

Nick groaned. "Oh, God, Cyndi, are we back to that again? You didn't cause Sonny's death. He did. He made the choice to get on that motorcycle. Maybe he was angry with you. If I remember correctly, I was mad at the whole world when I was that age. And I was selfish enough to want my own way all the time, too. Maybe you taught Sonny his first grown-up lesson—that he couldn't have everything he wanted. If he couldn't deal with that concept, if he went off half-cocked and reckless, then it was his problem. Not yours."

"All I know is I let him down."

Nick made a dismissing gesture. "Fine. Believe that if you have to. But stop dragging it into our lives."

"But it's a pattern of mine, don't you see? I'm always disappointing someone. My mother, who never thought anything I did was good enough. My husband, whom I never satisfied in bed or out. With you it's only a matter of time.''

"What are you expecting to do?"

"Disappoint you. Screw up the show. Not make you happy."

He stepped close to her, his eyes narrowing as he brushed knuckles across her jaw. "I hope you do disappoint me, Cyndi. I want you to make me sad. And angry. Just as I want your passion, the same way I want to hear you laugh and see your smile every single morning of my life. I want the full range, you see, the human range. With you, I'm willing to tip off the scale at both ends."

"I know that," she whispered, her voice husky. "You want everything, Nick. Sometimes I think it's more than I have to give."

"You're making the choice."

"If it were a choice I would change it."

"You *can* change it." Tunneling his hand through her hair, he tilted her face up to his. "Stop being afraid to be human, Cyndi. You're not this perfect little doll who never upsets anyone, who never makes any demands."

"That's the way I've always felt I should be."

"But I don't want that. I want a woman who's warm and real and willing to share her strengths and weaknesses. Beautiful dolls are cold and plastic and not very interesting."

"Oh, Nick." She stepped into his arms, drawing a shuddering sigh that trembled all the way through her body and was absorbed by his. "Nick, I want to be all those things for you."

He pulled back. "That's the problem, Cyndi. You want to be something for someone else. You should want all those things for yourself."

"I do," she insisted.

"Then prove it." The force of his love for her made him impatient. Weeks of frustration went into his next plea. "Marry me, Cyndi."

Her face freezing, she stared up at him.

"Marry me," he repeated. "Live with me. Fight with me. Watch my hair finish turning gray. Sleep with me every night. Get a mortgage with me. Have babies with me. Let's build a life, Cyndi. Instead of playing at love, we'll make something that lasts."

She turned away. Her voice was shaky as she said, "Marriage, Nick? That's what you want?"

"If you love me, it's what you want."

"Marriage is a big step. I've been there, remember?"

"You were a child," he retorted. "Marriage is for grown-ups. It's what happens when two people can't think of not living without each other." He paused. "Or isn't that how you feel?"

"Of course it is," she replied. "You know that's what I really want."

"Then say it."

She frowned. "Say it?"

"Say you love me."

She hesitated, and Nick felt a pain squeeze his heart. "You can't tell me that, can you?"

The muscles worked in her throat, and her lips trembled.

Nick felt off balance, as if someone had kicked him in the knees. "What is it that happens when you admit you love someone? Does that put too much on the line for you? Is it too real?''

"It's not that," she protested.

"When are you going to face the facts?" he asked. "Love isn't simple or safe. Love isn't always pleasant. It isn't you dressed up in your ball gown with that boy you thought you loved taking you to the prom. When you love someone, there's always some risk of failure, Cyndi. I'm willing to risk it with you. Why can't you do the same?"

"If only it were that simple."

His chest was aching from the anger and the fear raging inside him. Anger, because she couldn't, *wouldn't* see what they could have together if she would only let it be. Fear, because he wasn't sure she would ever be able to give him the total commitment he needed.

He clenched his fists at his sides. "You told me that every time you gave yourself to a man, you got nothing in return. Well, I don't want you to give yourself to me. I want us to be together. Give and take, Cyndi, that's what it's all about. Can't you trust me to give you what you need?"

Her eyes bright with unshed tears, she said, "Of course I trust you, Nick."

"No, you don't." Turning, he stalked into the bedroom and seized his clothes from the chair where he had left them. Cyndi followed and stood in the doorway, watching him with big, heartbreakingly blue eyes.

"Don't leave," she whispered. "Stay. I don't want you to leave like this."

"There's no use," Nick muttered as he pulled on his pants. "If you don't trust me, we don't have a chance.

Trust is the better part of love. And if you loved me, you'd trust me. But you don't trust anyone.'' He jerked his shirt on. ''Oh, yeah, the people in your life haven't been exactly inspiring, but what that's made you do is stop trusting yourself. And that's the real problem. Right now, your heart is telling you what you need to do. I wish you'd trust it enough to listen.''

Not pausing to button his shirt, he stepped into his shoes and started toward the hall. When Cyndi called his name, he paused in the doorway, but he didn't look back. With all his heart he wanted to turn around, take her in his arms and tell her everything would be okay, that he understood, that he'd settle for what she could offer him. But he didn't. He couldn't cheat himself, cheat her of what they could have. It was time for Cyndi to face some hard truths.

''Someday,'' he muttered, still not looking at her. ''Someday, maybe you'll exorcise all those ghosts that haunt you, Cyndi. When you do, when you're ready for the kind of love I have to offer, call me.''

Then he left. And he drove away into the black night.

Much later that night, Cyndi sat in her car, listening to the waves crash against the same beach she had visited the day she met Nick. But just like that day, there was no respite for her problems here. Tonight there weren't even any teenagers to distract her or draw her down the paths of her memories. She was alone with the sand and the sea and the dark sky.

Over and over, she kept seeing Nick's powerful car speed away from her house. She had stood in her front doorway, listening to his tires squeal as he turned the corner at the end of her street. She had driven Nick away. He couldn't wait to get away from her fears and uncertainties.

Just like Sonny.

As she once again made that connection, she tried not to give in to her panic. Nick wasn't like Sonny. He hadn't driven away, never to return. He couldn't have. She just couldn't survive if Nick disappeared from her life.

In admitting that to herself, she realized how much she loved him. She loved Nick. She could say those words to herself now, even though she hadn't been able to admit them to Nick earlier. And it was exactly for all the reasons he had named. Because loving him, loving anyone, was such an incredible risk. Because she didn't believe herself capable of living up to that risk.

And now she had ruined everything. She had hurt Nick deeply. Too deeply. What could she do? She couldn't just run to Nick with a declaration of undying love. No, not after everything they had said to each other tonight. He'd never believe her, never really trust her. And could she blame him? She didn't trust in herself, so how could she expect Nick to trust her?

For the first time since she had stopped believing that prayers worked, Cyndi raised her eyes to the sky and prayed. She prayed for Nick. And for herself. For the awful mess she had made of things. She prayed that somewhere there was a power strong enough to heal the rift she had caused between herself and Nick.

She never thought of taking Nick's advice, of looking to her own heart for the answers.

* * *

Dawn was just streaking the sky outside high, dusty-paned windows when Nick heard footsteps. He sat up as a bright light came on overhead. His solitude had come to an end.

"I'm over here," he said.

Sweet Pea jumped in surprise, turning from the bank of light switches to the bench where Nick had spent the past few hours. "Lawsy-day, Nick, you scared the fool outta me. The lights were out, so I didn't think anyone was in here."

"Sorry."

Still grumbling, the man came toward him. "What're you doin' here? How'd you get in?"

"Sweet Pea, you keep the key to the back door in the same place you and Dad kept the key to the gym back home. This isn't the kind of neighborhood for that. Someone other than me may be waiting for you some morning."

Grunting a little and rubbing his knees, the older man took a seat beside Nick. "Well, you know how it is, I've got these friends. Sometimes they need a place for the night. I like to leave the key where they'll find it."

"Yeah, I know. You're just like Pop," Nick said. He knew these friends of Sweet Pea's. Hollow-eyed, down-on-their-luck men, they were the same sorts his father had often given a free meal and a warm place to sleep. Pop had never turned his back on a buddy. Neither did Sweet Pea.

"You still haven't answered me," Sweet Pea continued. "What're you doin' here?"

Nick shrugged. Even to someone who had known him since childhood, it was hard to admit the sentimental feelings that had drawn him to this gym. Last night, after leaving Cyndi, he had wanted more than anything to talk to his father, to ask his advice. Not since those first months after Pop's death had he missed him with such intensity. By coming here to the gym, smelling the liniment-scented air, feeling the slap of leather-gloved fists against the punching bag, he had hoped to find something of his father's wisdom. Big, burly Tony Calderaro had always known how to help his son.

"Yeah," Sweet Pea murmured beside Nick. "I miss him, too, sometimes."

"How'd you know I was thinking of Pop?"

The older man shrugged. "I knew him. I know you, too." Silently he studied Nick's face. "Somethin' botherin' you, son?"

"Just wondering when my luck with women is going to change."

Sweet Pea chuckled. "Women. Oh, Lord, Nick. Women'll wear you out if you spend all your time worryin' about 'em. I take it from your state that I can put my tux back in the mothballs for a while."

"Probably forever," Nick returned glumly. "What do you do to make it work, Sweet Pea? You were married a long time. How'd you manage it?"

"I prayed a lot." Pushing his stocky frame off the bench, Sweet Pea shook his head. "That's all you can do, son, just pray it'll all work out, then go make it happen." He started to leave, then turned back. "I think that's what your father would tell you, Nick." Sweet Pea's grin flashed. "I know for a fact he did some powerful prayin' about your mother. Then he always went home to her.''

Nick returned the smile and watched his old friend amble away. Sweet Pea's steps were slower, his hair grayer, but he was so much of what he had always been that it wasn't hard for Nick to imagine his father walking by his side.

Feeling oddly comforted, Nick raised his eyes to the window where the morning's first sunlight was beginning to seep into the gym's gray interior.

And he took the advice his father might have given. He appealed to a higher authority for some help with Cyndi.

The going home to her, well, that took a little more thought.

Chapter Eleven

"You look like hell."

Swinging her front door all the way open, Cyndi said, "Gee, thanks, Lin. You know how to make a girl's day." She knew the tights and leotard she wore had seen better days, just as she was aware that her hair was disheveled, her face pale and full of strain. But she didn't care.

Lin gave her another considering glance. "Well, it is Saturday. I guess you're allowed to look that way."

"Is that supposed to make me feel better?" Turning on her heel, Cyndi went back to the living room, leaving her friend standing in the doorway.

Lin shut the door and followed her, taking a seat on the couch while Cyndi turned off the music to which she had been exercising.

"Did it help?" Lin asked.

Cyndi looked up from the CD she was sliding into its holder. "What?"

"The exercise. Did it clear anything up for you?"

A few weeks ago, Cyndi might have begun by denying there was anything to clear up. But she had grown tired of pretensions, especially with people like Lin who didn't expect them. So she shook her head, put the CD away and sprawled in the chair across from Lin. "I believe it would take more exercise than I'm capable of to make me feel any better about what's going on with Nick."

"So you two really had a big one."

"*The* big one. The end, I guess. I haven't seen him since night before last."

"He wasn't in his office yesterday."

"I know."

"So you tried to see him?"

"No," Cyndi murmured, shifting in her seat so Lolita could jump up beside her. "I just called his secretary to make sure he was okay. She told me he wouldn't be back in until Monday." Cyndi didn't share the visions she'd had of his sleek black Porsche going off the side of the road.

Lin settled back into the cushions, running her hands up and down her blue-jean-clad thighs. Finally, when the silence had stretched for several minutes, she said, "Do you want to talk about it?"

Frowning, Cyndi scratched her cat behind the ears. If she looked at Lin right now, she was afraid she might dissolve into tears. Her emotions were that close to the surface. "We've already discussed it, Lin. I'm just not up to a relationship with Nick. I can't give him what he wants or be what he needs."

"Is that what he says?"

"It's what I think."

"And so you just give up."

Instead of answering, Cyndi dropped her gaze to the floor.

"I think that's stupid," Lin pronounced.

"I do, too." Cyndi looked up as Devlin strolled in from the kitchen. "Sorry for eavesdropping, Sis, but I figured you might talk to Lin and I'd find out what was going on with you and Nick. You wouldn't talk to me last night." He turned to the other woman. "Cyndi's been moping around the house for the past two days. She's depressed even me."

"Tell me about it." Lin sat forward. "You should have seen her at the studio yesterday. She was in a fog, an absolute fog. I figured I'd better come check on her today."

"Thank you both for your concern," Cyndi said carefully, still afraid she might cry at any moment. "But I don't want your sympathy and I don't want to talk about Nick." She got up, thinking of going to her room.

Grasping her shoulders, Devlin pushed her back into the chair. "Now what is this about Nick? Something about not being what he needs?"

"Dev, just leave it alone."

He ignored her. "Where do you get these stupid ideas, anyway?"

Cyndi frowned up at her brother and glanced at Lin, who was perched on the edge of her seat, as if she was expecting some life or death pronouncement. "All right," she said. "Since you guys insist on prying, I'll tell you—Nick asked me to marry him."

"Oh, wow," Devlin said in mock horror as he sat down on the couch. "That's exactly what I'd do with a woman who doesn't fulfill any of my needs or wants."

"I can't marry him," Cyndi said. "Marriage just isn't for me. I've already proved that."

Lin held up a hand. "Wait a minute. Is Nick even remotely like your ex-husband?"

"No," Devlin spoke up. "Take it from me, Nick is nothing like the football star."

Her frown deepening, Lin said, "So, Cyndi, why do you think marriage to Nick will turn out the same way?"

There was something familiar about Lin's argument, something Cyndi didn't want to confront. She went back to her usual excuses. "It isn't that Nick is different. It's that I'm the same."

"Hold it right there," Lin said. "You're not the same as you were last year, Cyndi. You've changed almost every day since I met you. Just look at the way you've grown professionally. You were willing to stretch yourself, to take a risk and agree to the new show. That isn't the Cyndi Saint whose exercise show I first directed. And I'm glad to see it. Life without risk is pretty damn boring."

Lin's sentiment was awfully close to what Nick had told her. Too close, Cyndi thought, shifting uncomfortably in her chair.

"She's right," Devlin agreed. "You were even willing to try a relationship with Nick. When you broke off with that guy you were dating last year, I wondered if you would ever try again."

"Okay, okay," Cyndi said, throwing up her hands. "So you two think I'm a changed person. That doesn't mean Nick and I are right for each other."

"He must think so," Lin said quietly. "Otherwise, why would he want to marry you?"

That made even more sense. But just as she had resisted two nights ago, Cyndi wasn't giving in so easily. "It doesn't matter—"

"You're right," Devlin cut in. "All that really matters is that you love Nick. Do you?"

Lacing her fingers together, Cyndi tried to summon a negative response. But she couldn't. She loved Nick. That was a fact. She didn't know what to do with that love; she didn't know how it would solve any of her and Nick's problems. But there was no use hiding how she felt from the two people who were waiting so expectantly for her answer.

"I guess I do love him," she admitted. Just saying the words out loud sent a strange tingle through her.

Lin beamed. "You love him. He loves you. Is there still a problem?"

"Like we've said before, love doesn't solve all the problems."

"And as you told me once, isn't the man you love worth fighting for, worth working through the problems with? It was pretty good advice. I'm taking it, anyway."

Devlin's smile was teasing. "Gosh, Sis, did you tell Lin that? It sounds almost logical. You ought to consider following your own advice."

Cyndi stared at him and then at Lin, wondering why things that had seemed so complex just days ago were now so simple. Nick had told her where the answers were. He said she should listen to her heart. If she had believed him, trusted him, she might have been spared the anguish of the past few days.

Getting to her feet, Lin said, "I think my mission is complete here. So I'm going to have a late lunch with the man I love."

Devlin followed her to the door, offering to set up some wagers on likely wedding dates. Cyndi remained in her chair and tried to work up the courage to reach for the phone and call Nick.

Her brother came back into the living room just as a fresh onslaught of hesitation gripped Cyndi. She looked up at him. "Do you think Nick really loves me, Dev?"

His usual grin noticeably absent, Devlin ruffled her hair. "Who wouldn't love you?"

"I could give you a list in case you've forgotten my string of failures."

"Duds. All of them duds." Devlin shoved his hands into the pocket of his colorful shorts and rocked back on his heels. He looked more like the boy who had bedeviled her childhood than the man he was. "None of them were ever good enough for you, Cyndi. You just couldn't realize that. I never understood why you settled for so much less than you were worth."

"Maybe I haven't always been a prize, either."

"Hey, you're my big sister, the golden girl of Hazelhurst High. You always deserved the best." With a last, rather awkward touch on her arm, Devlin left Cyndi alone with her thoughts and the waiting telephone.

She went to her room. And in the mirror over her dresser, she stared at her reflection, trying to see herself as the important people in her life seemed to. Okay, so she was successful. She had a high-profile career. That could change tomorrow if the show failed. And she'd be very upset. But somehow, somewhere deep inside, Cyndi knew she'd bounce back if the worst happened. As Nick had taught her, she was learning to roll with the punches.

He had also taught her about passion. He had shown her she wasn't cold. She wasn't the frightened young girl Sonny, in his callow, youthful way, had so brutally rejected. She'd never have any reason to doubt herself in that respect again.

Still looking in the mirror, Cyndi raised her chin. She thought of that long-ago spring, when she had faced another mirror and seen only her mother's disapproval. Perhaps she had never stopped seeing her mother peering over her shoulder. It was time to see herself through her own eyes. Fran Saint's critical outlook, her impossible expectations had held her daughter back long enough.

"Maybe I've grown up," Cyndi murmured.

Once, she had been the "golden girl," as Devlin put it. She had been so certain of what turns her life would take. But nothing had happened the way she expected. Once she had regretted her choices and yearned for the certainty of the past. She hadn't been satisfied with who she was. But no more. It was funny how, for all her life, she had wanted to choose the safe route, and for some reason she always wound up on the dangerous path.

Nick was dangerous. Choosing a life with him would mean ups and downs, the "full range" of living he had told her he wanted. Loving Nick would never be safe or simple, would always be an adventure.

An that was exactly what Cyndi wanted. Being completely, totally sure of what she wanted was a wonderful feeling. Now she knew what to do with the love that was overflowing her heart.

She looked once more at the phone, but instead of calling Nick, she picked up her keys and headed for the garage. And her car almost collided with his in the driveway.

She fairly erupted from her car. With heart singing and laughter bubbling up from inside, she went flying to meet him. "You're here," she said unnecessarily. "I was coming to you, but you're here."

Nick took two steps forward and brought her into his arms. He hugged her. Hard. This wasn't how he had planned to greet her. He had planned to be very calm and logical, loving but firm. But he hadn't counted on the way she had run toward him, with her arms opened wide, her beautiful face alight. But then, he had never counted on Cyndi. From the beginning, she had been a surprise.

"I love you," she whispered, clutching him closer. "I love you, Nick Calderaro—completely, irreversibly. The way you said you love me."

He closed his eyes and held on to her, afraid if he let go she'd disappear like all the dreams he'd had of her for the past two days.

But Cyndi drew away and he looked down at her. Instead of disappearing, she said, "I prayed you'd come back."

Two prayers—answered.

Smiling, Nick sent a thank-you up to the heavens.

He touched her hair, kissed her sweet, willing lips. "I don't know how I survived the last two days."

"Me, either."

With fierce tenderness, he said, "I need you, Cyndi. I have to have you in my life. That's what I finally realized today while I sat in that apartment missing you. On any terms, I need you with me."

"There's only one set of terms," she replied. "There's only one way to really love someone. It's the way you offered me. I should have seen that, but I was too caught up in the same old fears that have always held me back."

"You're not now?"

She took a deep breath and tightened her arms around him. "I think I've got it all in perspective now."

"The past is over," Nick continued. "I can't ask you to not be affected by what happened before I walked into your life, but I want you to put the memories aside, Cyndi."

"I've already begun."

"I'm not going to hurt you like the others did."

"In my heart I was always sure of that."

His voice was husky as he asked, "So you trust me?"

"With my life."

It was so complete—the way she opened herself to him now. Nick found that amazing. "What happened? What's made you change your mind?"

Her eyes growing wide, her gaze swept over his face. She looked at him as if she didn't believe he was real.

"It started when I thought about spending the rest of my life without you. That's when I knew I loved you. Then Lin and Devlin helped me put all the rest of it in its proper place."

"Remind me to thank them."

"Thank me first." She kissed him. With fire and abandon, with the special kind of response that was Cyndi's alone.

Reluctantly Nick pulled away. This beautiful, vibrant woman wanted to share his life. He didn't know what he had ever done to deserve her. Touching her face in wonder, he said, "How could you ever doubt that you're everything I've ever wanted or needed?"

"It's easy to doubt others when you don't believe in yourself."

"That's what I want most of all. I want you to believe in yourself, Cyndi."

"Right now, I'm about as full of confidence as a woman can get."

Nick kissed her again. He put every bit of love he possessed into the kiss.

Finally, laughing, Cyndi pushed him toward the house. "Come on, let's stop giving the neighbors a show."

But Nick held her back and kissed her once more in the sunshine. That was what he always wanted for them. Sunshine. No shadows. Or doubts.

There was something in Cyndi's smile that told him he would get his wish.

Much later, moonlight filtered through the curtainless glass doors, brightening the bedroom. Cyndi lay, watching the play of light and darkness on the wall above her desk, listening to Nick's steady, sleep-evened breathing.

She felt so happy. So complete.

Her ghosts were at last put to rest.

Almost.

Carefully, trying not to disturb Nick, she slipped from bed. Lolita, curled in her new favorite spot against Nick's leg, meowed. Cyndi paused to stroke the cat's soft fur in reassurance.

Drawing on her robe, she went across the room to the desk. She lifted the blotter and pulled out the re-union invitation she had ripped in two so many months before. Something had kept her from throwing it away. With another furtive glance toward the bed where Nick was sleeping, she switched the desk lamp on to its dimmest setting and fitted the torn let-ter back together.

Instead of bad memories, the letter now brought only curiosity. Maybe she should go to the reunion, after all. It might be interesting to see what happened to the rest of Hazelhurst High. Was Ryder still a cocky firebrand? Had Meredith turned academia on its ear? Would Jennifer still have the same impossible-to-resist laughter? The desire to see her old friends swelled in-side Cyndi until she swiveled around in her chair and searched the middle shelf of the bookcase behind the desk.

Light glinted on raised gold letters, guiding her to her senior yearbook. She pulled it out and onto the desk. The pages fell open, as if by design, to a picture of Sonny. He was posed in his football uniform, his arm cocked back to throw a pass. The picture was faked, of course, and he wore no helmet, so his blond hair was ruffled by some long-ago breeze.

Hesitantly Cyndi allowed her fingers to trace over Sonny's youthful face. She knew a moment's sharp regret, but her heart didn't ache with loss, as it might have in the past. And instead of sadness, she thought of the pleasure she had known when Sonny smiled, the way he had pulled her ponytail in the second grade, that first kiss they had shared under a July sky.

It was true what Nick had said about Sonny the other night. He had been selfish. Spoiled, too. Used to getting everything he wanted. And maybe, just maybe, it wasn't her fault that he had died in that tragic accident. Perhaps it was all meant to happen the way it had. Sonny had been a comet, streaking across her life, across all of their lives. He had burned bright and fast, destined for only a brief appearance.

Cyndi touched his picture again. This handsome boy was a part of her past. And she was through looking back. She closed the yearbook. For now and forever, she was looking forward. With Nick.

"Hey," he called in a sleepy voice from the bed. "What are you doing?"

"Making plans," she said, and put the yearbook on the shelf where it belonged. "I think I'd like to take my fiancé to my high school reunion this summer. Think you can make it?"

Nick chuckled. "I'd rather you took your husband."

Cyndi stood, switched off the lamp and left her robe lying in a patch of moonlight as she approached the bed. "That could be arranged," she murmured, moving into Nick's waiting arms. "I think a wedding could most definitely be arranged."

*　*　*　*　*

Bubbly Jennifer Joyce was everybody's pal.
But nobody knew the secret longing she felt
for Sonny's best friend. . . .
Meet up with Jennifer, Cyndi
and Meredith this July,
in Erica Spindler's LONGER THAN. . . ,
Silhouette Special Edition #696,
the thrilling conclusion to
the SONNY'S GIRLS trilogy!

Silhouette Special Edition

presents

SONNY'S GIRLS

by Emilie Richards, Celeste Hamilton
and Erica Spindler

They had been Sonny's girls, irresistibly drawn to the
charismatic high school football hero. Ten years later, none
could forget the night that changed their lives forever.

In July—
ALL THOSE YEARS AGO by Emilie Richards (SSE #684)
Meredith Robbins had left town in shame. Could she ever banish
the past and reach for love again?

In August—
DON'T LOOK BACK by Celeste Hamilton (SSE #690)
Cyndi Saint was Sonny's steady. Ten years later, she
remembered only his hurtful parting words....

In September—
LONGER THAN . . . by Erica Spindler (SSE #696)
Bubbly Jennifer Joyce was everybody's friend. But nobody knew
the secret longings she felt for bad boy Ryder Hayes....